THE BEAR IS STIRRING

ANOTHER SPY STORY
By Peter Marshall

AUTHOR'S FOREWORD

The various characters in my first three spy novels were still on my mind as international tensions between Russia and the West began to deteriorate during 2022. It seemed that in these troubled times, there was clearly scope for a further story to be developed around the secret underworld of the intelligence and espionage agencies which I had written about in *"The Russian Lieutenant"*, *"Beyond the Funeral"* and *"There Are No Coincidences"*.

And this is it!

How the current geopolitical and military conflict will develop in the coming months, and even years, is anybody's guess. But the Russian "bear" is certainly stirring in many ways, and some aspects of this may be found in microcosm here in these chapters?

Writing spy fiction is a great release from the disciplines of my career in journalism and from the need for meticulous research of facts for the non-fiction books I have also authored and edited in my retirement years. I was fortunate to have worked in the USA for some 14 years, and to have travelled to many parts of the world on business –

all of which has helped me to provide a background of real life experiences as I allow my imagination to develop these fictional events.

This time, there is an assassination in Washington DC, a kidnapping in Moscow and incendiary bombs in the UK — plus an unexpected romance and a tragic ending in Scotland.

Once again, I am indebted to "anonymous" friends with relevant experience for their comments and insights (and the book title!) as they read drafts of this story for me. I hope the end result will prove to be enjoyable for readers, as well as thought-provoking.

Peter Marshall, Torquay, Devon, 2022.

Chapter 1

The VIP Flight

A US Air Force Learjet took off from the Yokota air base near Tokyo and climbed out over the Pacific Ocean into the bright rising sun – "a symbolic start to the day", thought the CIA chief as he took in the view, relaxed with a black coffee and contemplated the major achievements made during the past few days in Japan.

There were just five passengers enjoying the comforts of the luxury aircraft on the long flight, which began with seven hours over the expanse of the Pacific Ocean to the Hickam US Air Force base in Hawaii for a short overnight stopover; and then they would fly onwards to Washington DC with another rest and refuelling break scheduled at the Edwards US Air Force base in California. And during the long hours and time changes, each of them had very different things on their mind.

Bob Smithers, the Operations Director at the CIA, was in the front passenger seat, now relaxed in a white golf shirt with its Congressional Club logo, plus blue jeans and sneakers. In the previous few days, he had led his team on a successful mission in Japan to successfully discover the source of a leak of highly secret US Government information from inside the military communications centre in the island of Okinawa. It had been a great relief to have been able to report to Washington that the US Army "mole" was now in custody with the military police while the investigations continued. He was hopeful of a rapid conviction and with it an end to the widespread problems the leaks had caused.

During his six-day visit to Japan, Smithers had also successfully enticed a former Russian secret services agent serving as naval attache at the Tokyo embassy to "switch sides" – but he was still considering what he would plan next for the immediate future of the ex-spy who was now on board the same aircraft, sitting with two military escorts in the rear seats!

Bob's long time personal assistant Bettina was alongside him as usual, poised ready with her tablet and secure phone, prepared for the usual bombardment of instructions from her boss. She was relaxing in a blue tracksuit as she dealt calmly with the usual series of incoming messages arriving for the Director over the encrypted network from The Company's headquarters at Langley in Virginia. She was specially appreciating the smooth flight and she was able to ignore the fact that she was not a 'good flier', especially in small aircraft, and was liable to be feeling air-sick before long.

There were four empty seats behind them, providing some privacy, and then in the three rear seats were the two military police squaddies - a young corporal and an even younger private - in their smart blue dress uniforms. Seated between them was the stranger they had been instructed to escort to the USA. This came as a complete surprise to them at their army base near Tokyo the previous evening when they were told that they had been assigned to make this unexpected flight by their thoughtful commanding officer. These two were chosen because they were not among the majority of those on the base who lived there with their families during the overseas posting. Instead, they would be able to have a surprise visit back to their homes and friends in the USA for the Thanksgiving holiday before taking a regular commercial flight back to Japan a week later. They had also been carefully selected because they both had homes within easy reach of Washington DC, and they could not believe their luck as they settled into the comforts of an executive jet for the first time.

Meanwhile, their current task was to safely escort the man seated between them – a man called Nikolai Aldanov. They had taken charge of him at the Yokota air base early that morning and were told only that he was a Russian, that he was definitely not a prisoner, but that it was important that he should arrive safely in Washington where he would be handed over to an officer from the CIA. They quietly shared their surprise that when he boarded, he was not carrying any sort of baggage. But during their military police training, they had learned to expect the unexpected and not to ask questions.

Once they were at cruising altitude and had all settled comfortably on board the aircraft, the soldiers soon discovered that their charge Nikolai spoke good English with a foreign accent. They also found that he was equally discrete when asked casually about his background or the reasons for his flight to the USA. Their occasional conversations were mainly about the luxury of the aircraft and the progress of their long flight, with frequent interruptions by the flight steward, who introduced himself as Dwain. He was clearly experienced in recognising the needs of important passengers and responding politely. He knew when to emerge from his section at the rear of the plane to serve the flyers with drinks, food and various snacks, together with newspapers and magazines. And during the three stages of their long journey, he was also ready to provide blankets and pillows as they were needed for periods of sleep, as well as headsets and remote controls for the individual TVs.

Most of the time, the two young soldiers and their mysterious charge just relaxed, watched TV channels and made sure they enjoyed all the unexpected VIP services as the hours and time-changes passed by.

Meanwhile, Bob Smithers stayed busy at the front, dealing with matters back at HQ on the confidential satellite link and dictating a series of memoranda to Bettina. She was able to transmit these from the aircraft to various addressees at Langley and also to the State department and the White House in Washington DC. Staying busy took her mind away from any feelings of air-sickness and she did not get much opportunity to relax during the first stage of the flight to the US Air Force base near Honolulu. There, in a comfortable and well-equipped rest area, the group had time for a four-hours break with snacks and drinks plus couches for a brief sleep. When the aircraft eventually took off again, the work pattern continued for the busy CIA couple at the front while Aldanov and his escorts agreed that they had never expected to visit the Hawaian island, even for a few hours. They made the most of the aerial views, taking photographs on their I-phones as the plane made its descent and again as they departed.

There was another first experience for them when, at the appropriate stage in the flight, the pilot announced that they were crossing the international dateline, informing his passengers: "That's the end of yesterday – now it is tomorrow."

After a few more hours over the Pacific Ocean, Bob Smithers decided to catch some sleep before the aircraft arrived at the next brief stop-over in California – and Bettina was able to relax too. It was not until they took off again over the US mainland that he decided to move to an empty pair of seats behind them and he called Aldanov to come forward to join him.

"Well, you are in the United States now, so welcome," he began cheerfully. "How are you feeling after that early start today?" Aldanov replied cautiously that he was tired but otherwise okay, but he soon became more alert as the CIA boss told him: "That's good. You may not remember it now, but I am with the US Intelligence service. So are you ready to start working with us as we discussed in Tokyo?"

"Yes, of course, sir," the Russian replied, speaking carefully in his best, slow English. Striving hard to overcome his tiredness, he shook his head with disbelief as he continued: "But this has all happened so quickly, sir, that I am not really sure about what you have in mind. What I do know is that your organisation is very efficient and professional." He paused and then added: "Anyway, I don't think I have any alternatives."

"No, I guess not. But we will look after you," came the reassuring reply from Bob Smithers who went on to ask the Russian: "Have you been to the States in any of your previous lives?"

"Not exactly," said Aldanov, now sounding more confident. "But during my days in the navy, I once viewed the Florida coastline from on board my ship. I was an officer on a frigate and after exercises in the Atlantic, we visited Cuba for a few days and cruised past the American coast as well as Puerto Rica on the way. But I never thought I would actually get there, and certainly not this way – in a luxury aircraft".

"Well, I hope you were outside our territorial waters or we might have sunk your ship," commented Bob Smithers with a laugh, before continuing: "Looking ahead, I know that we can make good use of your experiences in the coming months. We have a special section at our headquarters near Washington which concentrates on Russian activities, and they have been briefed to expect a new addition to the team. After you have settled in, I am planning to base you there and it is a great help that you also speak the English language so well. Everything is totally confidential and top secret of course, and I am sure you will have some experiences to share with our experts there."

"Yes, I expected something like that," replied Aldanov. "It will all be new to me of course, but I am worried that the GRU may be able to track me down when I am there? They are pretty good, you know".

"Yes, I do know," came the quick response. "But we are better. Our first task will be to find you a new name and change your appearance. And we will also give you a set of new identity documents and so on – but you will be staying under close cover with us for a while."

Aldanov said he understood and smiled as the CIA chief then added: "So I guess it may be a few months yet before you can see a bit more of Florida close up."

They relaxed and enjoyed this comment as the CIA man described how some of the special units of the agency were actually in the sunshine state. He then went on to explain that when the aircraft arrived at their destination, they would be at an air force base a few miles from Washington DC where a car would be waiting to take him on the 1-hour drive to the CIA headquarters in Langley, in the state of Virginia. There would be no formalities for him to worry about and he would soon be in his new quarters on the base to have a meal and a good night's sleep.

The discussion was clearly over and Aldanov stood and said a polite "Thank you, sir" before he went back to his assigned seat at the rear of the aircraft. His two escorts could see that he was now more relaxed and cheerful, and he joined them in some banter about what he could expect in the USA and the pleasures of flying VIP. "I guess I will never do this again until I am a 4-star general," quipped the American corporal, looking thoughtfully at his one-way coach class ticket for the long flight from Washington back to Tokyo a week later.

Chapter 2

Finding Aldanov

"Where the hell is that man Aldanov," growled Yuri Bortsov, Director of the 5th Directorate of the GRU, Russia's secret intelligence service, at an early morning meeting with his senior staff at The Diamond, the modern Moscow headquarters of his department of Russia's Defence Ministry. This studious-looking and thoughtful academic, still in his late-30's, had only recently been promoted to the key responsibilities which he realised had once been the province of Vladimir Putin, no less. He composed himself and continued: "I have to report to the Minister later today and I know that will be his first question. Let's get our bureau chief in Tokyo on the line and we will try to put together what we know?"

So far, the group had only seen copies of a routine daily situation summary from the embassy in Japan, which Bortsov knew would also have reached the Minister's desk. It began with one eye-catching paragraph:

"The naval attache Nikolai Aldanov gave evidence in the Tokyo court yesterday where two Japanese men were charged with the attempted murder of two members of the Embassy staff last month in a shooting incident at a local bar. Aldanov, who has

recovered well from the injury he sustained in the incident, failed to return to the Embassy today and we are making further inquiries together with the Japanese authorities."

This information had alerted Bortsov, who knew more about the background to Aldanov's posting to Tokyo than the others in his team. And it had been the Minister himself who had made the decision to remove Aldanov from his position as a GRU officer based in Moscow and to downgrade him to the relatively obscure job as naval attache in the Japanese Embassy.

It was the culmination of a series of events which had all started many months earlier when Aldanov, then training to be an agent in the organisation, came up with the idea of putting his image on an international dating website – posing as a naval officer - hopefully to find a useful contact. The agency director was cautious, but eventually approved this interesting new initiative from his most recent recruit. Aldanov began by devoting a few minutes at the end of each day to checking responses on the website and after about two weeks, he was surprised to find one from an attractive-looking English woman, Marina Peters. She wrote in her on-line blurb that she had opened his entry on the website because she had Russian ancestors. As he read on, her reply became even more interesting when she revealed that she actually worked for the British navy at their Portsmouth base in England. Aldanov reported these details to his director, and he was even more pleased when it was agreed that he should tentatively follow up this new contact.

Aldanov had served as an officer in the Russian Navy for eight years before he took an opportunity to sign off and join the

Ministry of Defence Security Service for training to become a secret agent in the GRU. As he pursued his on-line relationship carefully over the next few weeks, he developed a plan whereby he would find his naval uniform again and join the crew of the next ship due to visit the UK. His director was intrigued by this initiative and the potential it offered for gaining contact with a new informant in the British navy – and especially one with a Russian family background. And so he approved the plan and worked with the Ministry logistics section who set up arrangements for Aldanov to join the crew of a Russian destroyer, the Admiral Essen. This was conveniently one of three ships due to sail from the Black Sea port in the next month on exercises, firstly in the Mediterranean and then the Atlantic Ocean, followed by a refuelling visit to Portsmouth. This looked perfect and so it was "Lieutenant Aldanov" who put on his uniform and travelled to the naval base at Sevastapol – it was like old times for him!

The on-line relationship continued with regular exchanges and it had developed into a budding romance by the time that Aldanov eventually met Marina on the dockside in Portsmouth. They set off on a tour of the city and enjoyed dinner together before ending the day at her seafront apartment. The pair were unaware that their lengthy cyber-romance had also been monitored by British intelligence – and that two MI5 agents were also at the dockside to observe their rendezvous. They were followed closely for the rest of the day until finally, in the late evening, the agents broke into the apartment, found them together in bed and arrested them.

The Russian was charged with espionage and breaches of security and at a short hearing in the Portsmouth court, he was remanded to await trial in London. It was decided that Marina had not committed any offences and, more importantly, that she would be a key witness at the forthcoming "show trial" of Aldanov for spying. The story of the brief romance became headline news about "The Russian Lieutenant and Marina" and she became a target for worldwide media interviews. She was also a target for Russia's GRU, who sent a pair of secret agents from London to Portsmouth with instructions to either influence her evidence or even prevent it. But MI5 were awake to this risk and rapidly decided to keep her safe until the trial. They flew her secretly to the USA where she was assigned to a remote CIA language training base in Florida … posing as a new recruit with a new name and learning Russian.

Then, unexpectedly, the Kremlin decided to avoid further embarrassment of a trial by agreeing a secret "spy swap". They released a British diplomat who they were holding in house arrest on suspicion of breaching Russian security and there was more worldwide media coverage when as part of the spy exchange, Aldanov was flown back to face disciplinary action in Moscow, which led to his dismissal from the GRU and reassignment to the posting in Japan.

Since there was to be no trial, Marina Peters was quietly flown home from the USA after just three weeks and began to open the pile of correspondence from the mailbox at her Portsmouth apartment – and was suddenly smothered by white powder. She was able to call the emergency services and was rushed into hospital, where she was not expected to survive. The police inquiries revealed that the two GRU spooks, who had been seeking her in Portsmouth, had finally left a deadly package of Ricin poison in her mailbox.

But the creative minds at MI5's London HQ, led by Tom Spencer, the Operations Director had other ideas. A plan was rapidly hatched jointly with the CIA for a very sick Marina to be secretly flown overnight by medivac to an American military hospital in Germany which held a still secret supply of a newly-developed antidote for Ricin poisoning, until then never used on a live victim. She was to become a crucial "guinea pig".

Meanwhile, a 'mock funeral' took place in Portsmouth with naval honours and there were tributes from family and friends about the tragic loss of a talented young woman with a new career ahead of her. Yakov Rozovsky, a senior diplomat from the Russian embassy in London was there among the mourners and as the ashes were scattered into the Solent from the nearby sea wall, he came forward with a red rose - from Marina's "Russian Lieutenant". He was being watched closely by two senior MI5 officers, and as he walked away towards the nearby car park he was arrested and taken to the police HQ to be charged as an accomplice to murder. A month later, he was jailed for eight years at the Crown Court in Winchester.

Miraculously, the new Ricin antidote had proved successful and with a carefully monitored treatment programme, Marina slowly recovered in Germany and was eventually flown to the USA where she was "re-invented" by the CIA's 'new identity' team in California for a new life as Samantha Lord.

It was the MI5 secret service chief, Tom Spencer, who arrested Aldanov in Portsmouth and then went on to be the architect of the creative events which led to Marina Peters' new second life. After a few months of training in the USA, Samantha Lord became a CIA operator, ready to undertake secret missions – but sadly unable ever to see her family and friends in Britain again. She carried out successful assignments in Mexico and Canada before being sent to join the agency's group in Tokyo for more experience and to join the team who were seeking a dangerous 'informer' at a US military base in Japan.

But her assignment was not a coincidence. MI5's sources discovered that as a consequence of the embarrassments that followed his romantic episode, he had been demoted and assigned to a minor role as naval attache at the Russian Embassy - in Tokyo. And so Tom Spencer developed another plan with his US counterpart, Bob Smithers. They agreed that in view of her background and possibly her past contact with Aldanov, "Samantha Lord" might be able to play a key role in important investigations into a leak of secret American information in Japan. She was sent to the island of Okinowa, where the most important US military bases were located and used her skills to follow a trail which led to the detention of an Army 'mole'.

Meanwhile, at the end of the first week of his new posting, Aldanov and his Japanese assistant Hideki Endo went out to explore the city - but they were unaware that they had been followed by two Japanese gunmen. When they went into a city bar, they were both injured in a shooting incident (which turned out to be a protest against the continuing and long-running dispute over Russia's occupation of Japan's Northern

Territories). During his recovery from a shoulder wound, Aldanov was called to give evidence in the trial of the gunmen.

The CIA chief, Bob Smithers, had also flown to Tokyo to oversee the investigations there. He created an opportunity through his Japanese contacts to secretly confront Aldanov while he was involved with the Japanese court system – and for Marina (now Samantha of the CIA) to then meet him face-to-face. He set up a dramatic one-on-one confrontation in the police station, where Marina insisted that he "owed her" for the near-fatal consequences of their on-line romance. He could hardly believe that she was actually the same woman he had last seen when they were arrested in her Portsmouth apartment. But she had departed too soon with her boss, and he spent a sleepless night recalling their brief romance and wondering how he could see her again?

But with typical subterfuge, the CIA boss followed through and when the court case ended, he planned an opportunity to intercept Aldanov the next day and, together with Samantha, to persuade him to switch sides.

And without any further delay, the Russian was whisked away on the secret flight to the USA early the next morning.

Chapter 3

Missing in Japan

And so it was that in Moscow the following day, the GRU Director Yuri Bortsov was alarmed when he read a further report from his Tokyo bureau chief. It informed him that the court case against the gunmen had been started and that Aldanov had disappeared. The day after giving his evidence, he had not returned to the Embassy and was therefore reported to the Japanese authorities as missing.

At his morning meeting with his key staff, Bortsov soon had the GRU bureau chief in Tokyo, Vitaly Livitsky, joining them on the line and he began with the key question: 'So tell me? Where is Aldanov now?"

Livitsky replied that he had no idea! And he went on to describe how two days earlier a Tokyo police car had collected Aldanov from the Russian embassy without any advance warning and taken him to the city courthouse to be a witness at the trial of the men who had attacked him. He had immediately sent one of his agents, Pavel Ilia, to 'keep an eye on Aldanov' but he had been unable to see him because he was involved in meetings with the prosecuting lawyers. He was then told that for security reasons the Russian would be remaining at the police house overnight accommodation and stay until he had given his evidence the next day.

He continued: "I then sent the same agent there again to watch Aldanov give his evidence when the trial commenced, and he watched until the lengthy hearing was adjourned. Eventually, Ilia found a very tired Aldanov in the adjoining police office and took him by taxi to his Tokyo apartment. Apparently, he did not say much to Ilia on the way, except that he had now been discharged as a witness. I told Ilia to stay on the job and early the next morning, he was waiting nearby when Aldanov emerged from his flat to walk to the embassy as usual and followed him."

In fact, Aldanov had been feeling pensive after the shock of meeting his Portsmouth date again in such a dramatic fashion the previous afternoon at the police court. And then, on his usual morning walk to the embassy through a typically wooded Tokyo park, he spotted a couple watching him as he approached a park bench. He could hardly believe it when the woman beckoned to him – and with a smile which he quickly recognised as his long lost English date yet again. He could not resist the invitation to join them.

In his report to Moscow meeting, Livinsky described how his agent Ilia had been following Aldanov until he reached a park and unexpectedly saw him sit on a bench to join a man and a woman. "But then", said the Tokyo bureau chief, "After only a minute or so, he says he saw two Japanese police officers arrive and they escorted the three people to a waiting car which drove off very quickly. That was the last we saw of Aldanov."

Bortsov snorted angrily and banged on his desk asking: "And he got away?"

Livitsky went on to describe how his agent had managed to use his phone to take one distant photograph of the three people sitting on the bench but he did not have time to get a picture of the departing car. The photograph had been studied with hazy enlargements of the three individuals together, but there was not sufficient clarity to identify them. He added that he had reported these incidents to General Malinov, the Ambassador in Tokyo, who was now pursuing the matter with his Japanese government contacts. In view of the involvement of the two Japanese police officers, he agreed that they should expect the authorities to provide assistance in trying to locate the whereabouts of Aldanov.

"This is not good. Keep me informed," said a very troubled Bortsov, who quickly closed the meeting and said he had to prepare for a meeting at the Ministry of Defence near the Kremlin. His car was called and he was punctual as usual. As he expected, the senior Deputy Minister, General Yazov, was waiting for him in his spacious office and after a brief greeting came the expected question about the missing diplomat in Tokyo.

After listening patiently to the story so far, the minister said: "I will wait for the Ambassador's report from Tokyo before commenting any further about this problem. I also want more information about the loss of our intelligence source in the American military there. It could mean another trial in the courts, in Japan this time, and more bad publicity which will upset the President's people".

Bortsov said he understood and added that he had actually inherited these problem.

"I know," said General Yazov. "But remember, we have other big problems in your area, too. There are two of your agents still in jail in London, arrested after hitting the wrong target last year. Then there is the diplomat in a British jail after being wrongly convicted of conspiracy to kill Aldanov's woman. And you also have two more experienced agents who are blacklisted from international travel after leaving Ricin in the same woman's apartment. I am also concerned about this mysterious new CIA woman your people have picked up.

"It is not a good scene and we need to take action," he insisted firmly, and then added: "Of course, I do know that most of these events happened before your time in the directorate Bortsov … but the problems go on. I want you to get a grip on the situation and bring me some good results. Okay?"

The GRU chief said firmly that he fully understood, and with a salute to the general, he departed to start working on a new plan. In his car during the trip back to The Diamond, he decided to begin with an immediate visit to Tokyo for a first-hand investigation into two of the problems at the centre of his new challenges.

Chapter 4

A Surprise for "M"

At the Thames-side headquarters of MI5 in London, Tom Spencer was back at his desk after a 3-weeks world tour to visit staff members based at seven different British embassies. In his long career with the secret services in both MI5 and MI6, he knew most of them well and enjoyed the opportunity to recall their past experiences and successes. As Deputy Director for Operations, he had worked closely with the team on many secret and important challenges. But this time, he was also visiting them to say 'goodbye and thank you' before his forthcoming retirement.

Waiting on his desk, his thoughtful secretary Celia had arranged a colourful display of welcome-back flowers, together with a file of messages from many of those he had met on his travels, wishing him well in the future. Before returning to his office, he had taken a couple of days off to settle back into his apartment in North London's Primrose Hill area and to recover from jet lag – but his in-tray could wait because he had stayed well up to date on current issues throughout his trip and would be having a departmental briefing to update him later in the day.

Also awaiting him was a phone message from his boss, "M", inviting him to meet for lunch at the Reform Club at 1pm He had a relaxed chat with Celia about his travels around the world and then joined his deputy in the adjoining office for a coffee before deciding that there was still time on this autumnal morning to re-acclimatise with a walk along the embankment from Vauxhall and then through St. James Park to Pall Mall. He was waiting in the elegant club lobby when he saw an official car arriving outside, and "M" strolled in, looking calm and relaxed as usual.

"Welcome back, Tom," he called out as he walked up the steps, also pausing to greet the friendly porter on the way. "I called to give you a lift, but you had already gone – come and have a drink".

After a convivial chat about his travels over a dry sherry in the bar, they moved to the reserved table in the spacious dining room next door and ordered from the menu – both choosing a fillet steak and agreeing to share a bottle of the club's house claret. "And so, what is the verdict, Tom," was the first direct question from "M", looking serious at last. "Are we in good shape around the world?"

"Nothing the guys cannot handle," came the reassuring reply. "But as you probably saw in the reports, there was an interesting episode when I was in Tokyo. That big Texan Bob Smithers from Langley showed up there, and we had a double success by discovering a mole in the American military and we also got a former Russian agent based at the embassy there to swap sides. I think they were planning to fly him back to the States the next day in Smithers' plane. So it was job done."

"Yes, I liked the sound of all that when I read the logs and I am sure you had some creative input as usual. So what is your plan now that you have spread the word about your retirement? It goes without saying that the service will miss you – and so will I. But it won't be for long in my case because while you were away, I took an opportunity to discuss my own retirement plans with the Permanent Secretary. As you know, I had already discovered that you were not in line for promotion to this job as I had hoped, and anyway, it is probably time for some new blood in the service. In any case, think we have both done more than our share over the years."

"Yes, you are right as always," said Tom, raising a glass of wine in a silent toast to the man who had encouraged and supported him over many years.

"You asked me about my plans", he continued, and then after pausing rather mysteriously, he added: "Well I have some more news for you because I am getting married – at last."

"M" dropped his cutlery noisily, gasped, and replied loudly: "What? Are you serious? Well, knowing you, I am sure you are, but tell me more?"

"Well, its s long story," Tom began. And the boss listened intently as Tom recalled his involvement in the Portsmouth Ricin poisoning event more than two years previously. He reminded "M" about the incident when a woman working for the British navy as a civilian had become involved with a Russian through an on-line dating website and how the Russian turned out to be a spy in naval uniform. "M" remembered it well and did not need to be reminded about the "Russian Lieutenant" headlines, the fake funeral and the risk that Tom had taken by arranging with the Americans for the testing of a new antidote for the Ricin poisoning of the woman involved.

"She was called Marina Peters as I am sure you remember," Tom continued. "And as I monitored her slow but amazing and complete recovery, I came to admire her strengths and her potential – among other things. Well, as you know, we completed our joint plan with the Americans by sending her to the States for training as an agent with the CIA and I stayed in touch as she took on a new persona as Samantha Lord. This was a name I actually invented for her – and she proved me right when she became involved in several secret operations and not surprisingly, I followed every step closely. I imagine you can now guess what is coming next?"

"Yes, I don't need to be a genius to guess that," said "M" with a chuckle. "When is the wedding?"

"First, there is another part of the story," continued Tom. "You may also remember that Aldanov, the Russian spy, avoided a court hearing for espionage when he was part of a Foreign Office swap with a British diplomat under house arrest in Moscow. Then he was then sacked from the GRU, demoted and sent to a quiet posting in Tokyo as naval attache. When I heard this, I arranged with Washington for Marina, now known as Samantha of course, to be moved to Tokyo for more experience. And if course, there was always the chance that she might eventually meet up with the Russian again and be useful in some way through her previous contact.

"So I was there in Tokyo when that major information leak from the American military in Japan cropped up and it was our Marina, now Samantha of course, who cracked it by tracking down the mole in Okinawa. And then she went on to work wonders when the CIA arranged an opportunity for her to meet the Russian again while he was at the police court before the case against the two Japanese gunmen. And now comes the romantic bit – not for the Russian but for me. Okay so far?"

"Yes, carry on, I am beginning to enjoy this," came the enthusiastic reply from "M" with a chuckle.

"Well, I am not sure what was actually driving my emotions," Tom went on, choosing his words carefully. "But I guess it began when I played a part in saving her life, then created her new persona. I certainly came to admire her strength of character during the months of tough training with the CIA. So when we met again at the Tokyo embassy, I have to say that I realised that I was smitten. She is a beautiful woman and I had never felt this way about anyone I have met in the past. So I arranged to meet her for dinner that evening at a smart Japanese restaurant with geishas and all that, and I tried to sense her feelings for me. I know it all sounds a bit premeditated, but I had an engagement ring in my pocket just in case and when I felt the moment was right I asked her to marry me. And what is even more important, she agreed."

"So congratulations, Tom," said his boss, raising a glass and then he called the waiter and asked him to bring two celebratory brandies. "There's clearly another side to you that I never saw over the years and if she is the right one for you, then I am so glad you have found her at last. I am sure you can enjoy a wonderful retirement together. You certainly deserve it. So when is the wedding?"

"There are a few things to sort out first," he continued. "With your approval, I need to start by working with Washington to have Marina quietly released from their system. They will need to deal with restoring her original identity so that she can return legally to the UK. I am sure they know how to handle it and how to ensure that Samantha Lord disappears quietly from the scene. Then when she has her British nationality again, I am thinking that she and I could have a spell together, maybe somewhere like Bermuda, to work out our longer- term future. Then I hope we can arrange a quiet wedding there in the island with just one or two friends."

"Go for it, Tom," said "M", convincingly. "As you probably know, you will be on our books here for another couple of months yet before your official retirement date. So I will make sure you have the time and resources to work everything out. Let me know if there is any way I can help, especially with the Americans".

And as they raised their brandy glasses one more time, the boss added: "By the way, Tom, I will certainly arrange to be in Bermuda for the big day – that is if I am invited, of course."

They strolled cheerfully out of the club and the Director's car was waiting by the door in the afternoon sunshine – and Tom was invited to join his boss for the trip back to the office. They were in a relaxed mood and a good day got even better when they walked out of the lift on the third floor to be met by Tom's assistant.

She handed him a brief, top secret message from Bob Smithers of the CIA, which he quickly shared with "M" - and they smiled knowingly as they read it:

"Am on my way back from Japan with Aldanov. Samantha fixed him – call me tomorrow."

Chapter 5

The Briefing

The GRU Director Yuri Bortsov, decided to start confronting his new challenges by flying out of Moscow on the first available Aeroflot flight to Tokyo. He left instructions that his bureau chief there should not be informed about his trip until he was able to confirm his arrival at Narita airport. And so he was already in a taxi on his way into the city when Vitaly Livitsky got a surprise message at 10 am to tell him that his boss was nearly there! He quickly assembled his team and asked them for any new information about the missing diplomat. There was none.

He went upstairs to the Ambassador's office and discovered that General Malinov had also received the same short notice of the surprise visitor from Moscow. He had already placed a call to his usual contact in the Japanese foreign affairs office, hoping for some new information to follow up on his call the previous evening concerning the missing diplomat and the involvement of the local police in his disappearance. They began to consider the options confronting them and were still waiting for the call to be returned from the Japanese ministry when they were interrupted by the Ambassador's somewhat flustered personnel assistant to say that Mr. Bortsov had arrived unexpectedly from Moscow.

"Bring him straight up here," said the General, then adding as an afterthought, "And bring us coffee for three and with vodka on the side."

It took a few minutes while the surprise visitor was shown to an adjoining bathroom to quickly freshen up after his long flight. Then as he entered the grand office, he saluted the Ambassador smartly and offered his apology for the lack of advance notice of his visit.

"No, no – you are most welcome Yuri Bortsov. And I am never surprised by the people from your section," said the Ambassador. "Come and sit down to relax with some refreshment after your long flight – and I am sure you know Vitaly Livitsky, of course."

They sat in three comfortable armchairs set around a low glass-topped table and coffee was poured for them by the Ambassador's assistant as Bortsov explained that he was quite new to the 5th Directorate and in fact had not yet met any of his overseas team, including Livitsky. But he said he was pleased to have a good reason to make this first trip and was looking forward to working with the agency's Tokyo group. "I have heard good things about you," he said convincingly to his local bureau chief.

"Let me begin by congratulating you on your new appointment, Yuri, if I may call you that," said the Ambassador. "And I know you are here because we have some important issues to sort out. Where shall we start?"

"It has to be this man Aldanov," replied Bortsov. "I know he is missing, so how much do you know about his local contacts and recent activities?" The Ambassador nodded his understanding and held out a hand to indicate that he wanted Livitsky to respond to the question.

Choosing his words carefully as he addressed his two bosses, the bureau chief began by saying that he assumed they both knew about Aldanov's history as a former GRU agent in Moscow and his ill-fated venture to try to recruit a British woman working for the navy. And then how he was removed from the secret services Directorate and sent to Tokyo as naval attache, only to become involved in a shooting incident in a local bar in his first week.

"Not a good start," the Ambassador interrupted. "But he was lucky to get away with just a shoulder wound and he was only in hospital for a few days. His Japanese assistant called Endo was with him and he had much more serious injuries and is still in hospital. So I have not seen very much of them in recent weeks and my administration manager has been staying in touch during this period. But I did get a message from the defence ministry in Moscow a week or two ago enquiring about Aldanov – was he recovering and how was he settling in of course. But it seemed to me that there were still some suspicions about him and it was suggested that we should keep a close eye on him. So I asked Livitsky to do just that".

"Yes. Two of my agents were assigned to check on Aldanov's activities but there was little to report", said Livitsky, picking up the story. "It seemed that he just walked from his apartment to the office every morning, checked his messages, chatted with the admin office about finding a replacement for Endo, read files until mid-day and then took the metro to the American club for lunch – pretty boring, it seemed. And then he either went sightseeing in the city or returned to his apartment for quiet evenings with his TV and his books. He had not yet received any new assignments from Moscow, but we checked his phone and on-line records and they showed nothing to be concerned about".

"That sounds reasonable so far," said the Ambassador and Bortsov said he had no questions so far and asked eagerly: "But what happened next?"

Livitsky continued: "I thought it all sounded a bit out of character for a man who had previously been active as a GRU agent, so I went to the American club myself the same day to see who he met there. Aldanov appeared to be alone in the bar until he spotted me and came to join me. As we chatted, I realised that he was getting restless about having very little to do now that he had stopped having regular medical treatment. He said he had visited Endo at the hospital a couple of times, but otherwise the only other thing he mentioned were a couple of sessions with the local police to give them statements and to answer their questions about that shooting affair in the bar. And then just two days later, we were very surprised to hear that he had been collected from the embassy by the Japanese police at mid-morning. We discovered that he was taken to the courthouse to

33

give evidence against the two gunmen charged with attempted murder."

"Did he tell anyone before he left?" asked Bortsov.

The Ambassador took up the story and replied: "It turns out that as he was leaving the building, he told the reception desk and the security man that they were going to the courthouse in the city about the shooting business. This was not a surprise, of course, and it all seemed quite routine to them and the information was not passed on to my office for more than an hour. I was rather concerned that we had no advance notice and so I took action straight away. I asked Livitsky to send one of his people to the courthouse to discover what was happening and I made an urgent call to the foreign office to lodge an official complaint. We should at least have had a few days advance warning about the start of the trial so that we could give some advice to Aldanov and arrange an interpreter. I set up an appointment with my senior contact there and took Livitsky with me to the government offices to find out what was going on.

"When we arrived, I found that we had an appointment with an under-secretary who I knew, but all we got was the usual polite bowing and introductions followed by an apology and a promise to respond with an explanation the next day. I told them him that this was very unsatisfactory," added the Ambassador with a growl.

Bortsov went on to ask what had been discovered by the agent who was sent to the courthouse and Livitsky replied that when Ilia arrived, he was told by the police that the case had been opened and adjourned until the next morning without taking any evidence. Meanwhile, the witness was being interviewed by the prosecuting lawyers and could not be interrupted.

Livitsky continued: "Ilia was told that Aldanov would stay at the adjoining police hostel overnight which was described as a normal procedure for an important witness to ensure that he could not be contacted or influenced by another party before giving evidence. So Ilia left and returned to the courthouse again early the next morning and eventually he was able to meet Aldanov in the police canteen, accompanied by his assigned Japanese interpreter. But he could not talk to him alone. Ilia was then in the courtroom for the hearing and it was a long day, all in Japanese of course so Ilia did not understand much of it until Aldanov gave his evidence through his interpreter. Then when he was eventually released, Ilia was able to take him back to his apartment by taxi."

"So is this man Ilia in the embassy today?" interrupted Bortsov. "It sounds like he must be the last person to see our man before this strange disappearance and I would like to hear his report first hand please?"

"Yes, of course. You will find that he is one my brightest young agents," replied Livitsky. "I will go to find him." As they waited, Bortsov and the Ambassador just looked at each other, clearly perplexed and saying little as they drank coffee and shot of vodka.

Chapter 6

Arrival at Langley

At the Andrews US Air Force base near Washington DC, two vehicles were waiting when the Learjet came to a stop at the end of the long flight from Tokyo. The first was a limousine, which quickly whisked away silently with the CIA chief, Bob Smithers, and his assistant. The second was a large black SUV with darkened windows from which a tall, serious-faced man in a business suit emerged. He warmly welcomed Nikolai Aldanov in Russian, introducing himself as David from the CIA and he led the way together with the two military police escorts to the waiting vehicle with its engine running. Without any arrival formalities to delay them, they were driven off at speed, eventually joining the traffic on the busy city beltway until they reached the Virginia Parkway exit. Aldanov was tired and bewildered, but he was relieved to be able to converse in his native language with David, who told him he was in charge of the CIA's Russian section. "We are a friendly team," he reassured the new arrival, adding: "It is really good to see you here safely and we will give you all the help you need to settle in with us, so don't worry about a thing".

It was mostly a quiet journey, apart from some occasional words about the weather and the traffic as Aldanov tried to sleep. After about an hour's drive in the afternoon sunshine, they arrived at the tree-lined entrance to the CIA's Langley headquarters. At the security gates to the Agency headquarters, a military sergeant was waiting for the two soldiers who had travelled from Tokyo. But first, the CIA man took them to one side and quietly reminded them that this had been a top-secret flight and that as members of the military police, they were bound by the official secrets regulations. "Yes, sir," they said smartly and in unison. And with their job completed, there was just some paperwork and instructions waiting for their return flights in due course. They were then driven back into the city to make their own way to their respective homes for an unexpected week's leave to spend the Thanksgiving holiday with their families.

Nikolai Aldanov was surprised and impressed to see the size of the central buildings and the number of other buildings spread around the campus. As they walked towards a smart, modern block, David explained that this was one of the residential facilities on the base where he would be able to relax for a few days. "We know you have arrived without any luggage or personal belongings, of course, and we can arrange to get anything you need as you settle in."

The Russian was impressed by the typical CIA efficiency when he was met by two members of staff waiting to take him to room B, which was a comfortably furnished suite with a single bedroom, a sitting room with TV, a modern and well-equipped bathroom and a small kitchenette. As he introduced his two colleagues, David explained: "Alexander is also Russian but he is now an

American citizen, of course, and he will be your liaison man for the next few days so ask him for anything you may need. And Annette here is from our housekeeping staff and knows where to find all your personal needs, toiletries, clothing items, food and drinks and so on."

Nikolai nodded his appreciation and said he really needed a bath and a long sleep after his journey – "But first just a light meal – some soup maybe and a coffee?"

It was obviously time for David to depart saying: "That's fine. You will be looked after here. Sleep well and I will see you tomorrow." And then Alexander and Annette went to work ensuring that the new arrival had everything he needed as quickly as possible. They soon produced some night clothes and toiletries and Annette aid she would return in a few minutes with a full set of clothes for the next morning. Before they left him to settle down, Alexander gave Nikolai a number to call if he had any questions and told him: "Your food will be brought here for you soon and unless I hear from you first, I will come to find you around eight in the morning to take you to breakfast."

Exhaustion ensured that he slept for nearly twelve hours and the bedside clock showed nearly 7am when he woke up and found that he could make coffee in the kitchenette to start his day. The sun was shining outside and from his window, Aldanov surveyed the scene around him, trying to adjust to the fact that his life had suddenly changed dramatically in the course of an unbelievable two days.

As he prepared himself for whatever the day ahead held for him, he reflected on his unexpected encounter with the English woman at the Tokyo police station and then his rendezvous with her again in the park with the CIA chief – and then, with mixed feelings, he remembered their day together in England.

"And it has all led to this," he mused. "So this is America – this is really the CIA - what next?"

Chapter 7

Ilia's Story

Pavel Ilia was looking nervous as he walked into the luxurious Ambassador's office for the first time. He was introduced by his bureau chief Livitsky, who pulled up another chair for him facing the group before explaining: "As you know Ilia, this is about Aldanov and it seems that you were the last person here to see him, so can you start by telling us what happened when you went to the courthouse on Wednesday afternoon?"

"Yes, of course," he replied, clearing his throat and choosing his words carefully. "There is a police department adjoining the courthouse and because I have not learned much Japanese yet, I showed my ID to the officer at the desk and in my best English explained that I was from the Russian embassy. He went away to find an interpreter and about ten minutes later, another officer arrived who spoke some English but not Russian. I was able to explain slowly and carefully that I was looking for one of our diplomats from the embassy called Nikolai Aldanov who I understood was at the courthouse. He just nodded and then disappeared for quite a long time, and I was left waiting in the reception area again.

"Eventually the interpreter returned with another man who appeared to be a more senior police officer and he explained that it was not yet possible for me to see my Russian colleague. He took some time to answer my questions, but he clearly knew that Aldanov was there and was a witness in an important case which had opened in the adjoining courthouse earlier that day. It had now been adjourned until the next morning and the witness was now involved in meetings with the prosecuting lawyers. Then he would stay overnight at the adjoining police hostel for his own protection and to ensure that he was not influenced by anyone. He described this as a normal procedure."

"Were they friendly to you?" asked Bortsov.

"Not particularly," came the reply. "I have never felt that Japanese officials are being friendly towards Russians like most other people are. But he ended by saying that I could be in the courthouse the next morning when my colleague was due to give evidence. He also suggested that if I could return there at about 8 am, he could probably arrange for me to spend some time with my colleague before the case began."

Ilia said it was then mid-evening, so he reported the situation to his chief by telephone and was told to return to the courthouse the next morning. He was there by 8am as suggested and was met by another bi-lingual Japanese police officer who took him to the police canteen where he found Aldanov already seated at a table.

"He gave me a warm and friendly greeting and he was clearly pleased to see a friendly face," continued Ilia. "But the interpreter stayed with us while we had coffee and some breakfast croissants. I was not sure how much the Japanese officer understood, so we could not have a relaxed conversation of course. I did not really know much about Aldanov anyway, but he reassured me that he was being treated well and said he had been told what to expect when the court hearing resumed at 9.30. In fact, he seemed quite relaxed about it and eventually, he was taken away by the police officer and I was shown the way into the observer seats in the court room. I could see Aldanov at the front with the lawyers and after the judge arrived, the two Japanese prisoners were brought into the dock by armed police officers. I thought they looked very young and frightened. When the case began, it was all very formal and lengthy and of course I did not understand any of it for nearly an hour until Aldanov was called to the witness box".

Ilia then described how a court interpreter was sworn in and said that from then on, all the exchanges were translated very slowly between Japanese and Russian. He said the short version of what followed was that Aldanov described in great detail all he knew about the incident involving himself and Endo in the bar.

"Eventually," continued Ilia, "Aldanov was questioned by the defence lawyer and asked to identify the two men accused of attempted murder. He insisted that he had not previously seen them, either before or after the shooting incident so he could not help. The judge and the lawyers then had a long exchange which, so far as I could tell, was about the best way to arrange to hear evidence from Endo in the hospital. And then Aldanov was called forward again and told, through the interpreter, that the case would be adjourned until Endo could give his evidence but that he was now released as a witness and would not be required any further by the court."

"Thank you, Ilia, that was very helpful," said Bortsov, clearly impressed by the detailed account from the young agent. "But what happened next is even more important because I gather you had a chance to talk privately with Aldanov."

"Yes, he had to go off to sign some documents and to collect his belongings, and then he was free to leave with me and we found a taxi outside," explained Ilia. "He said he was very tired after a poor night's sleep followed by the ordeal of the court hearing. So I called my chief who agreed that I should take Aldanov back to his apartment and arrange a meeting with him at the office first thing next morning."

Livitsky then asked: "That was about a 30-minutes taxi ride, I believe – so what did you talk about?"

"He was very quiet at first, which I understood of course," said Ilia. "But then he began to talk about my job and said how much he was missing his previous life with the GRU. He said that when he arrived at the Tokyo embassy, he had been told not to become involved with our department and he asked me what I thought he could do help him return to becoming an agent again. I think I made a joke of it by saying 'Once a spook, always a spook' and I wished him well, but I tried not to get involved.

"Then he told me that when he was in the American Club for lunch two days earlier, he had overheard someone saying that there was a CIA big-wig in town and also that there was an important investigation going on. He asked me whether it might help him if he passed on this information to the bureau chief? So I said that Livitsky probably knew all this anyway and that in the circumstances, it might be better if he kept a low profile and got on with his own job for a while. That was about it."

"Well done, Ilia", said Bortsov. "That was certainly a strange conversation, but I get the picture so far. So what happened the next morning?"

Ilia went on to describe in detail how he returned to the apartment block early, as instructed, and waited discretely for Aldanov to emerge: "Soon after 8.30, I saw him come out dressed in a business suit and tie and carrying his briefcase. He walked briskly for a few hundred yards and then crossed the road into a park area where several people were exercising. Aldanov was clearly not dressed to join the joggers, so I stayed a discrete distance behind as he walked on until he suddenly stopped and sat down on a park bench to join a man and a woman. I took one photo and could see they were in conversation, so I tried to approach closer behind some bushes to take a closer photo. But when I next looked, there were two uniformed Japanese policemen approaching them and very quickly they escorted all three of them to a car waiting a few yards away which then drove off at high speed before I could see any more. So I advised my chief by phone immediately and then returned here to report what I had seen."

Ilia then described how he was sent with the Embassy's administrative officer to search Aldanov's apartment and they found that all his personal belongings and his luggage cases were still there, but no documents of any kind could be found.

"Thank you, Ilia, that is all very clear," said Bortsov. "It seems that he was not expecting to leave permanently when he set off. But can you give any more detailed impressions of the two people he met in the park? And what might he have been carrying in his briefcase?"

"As my photo shows, they were both white and maybe middle-aged, dressed rather casually, and I am sorry but I did not get a chance to take a shot where we could see their faces clearly," replied Ilia, adding "And I cannot begin to guess what was in his brief case. He had not been in his office at the Embassy since he was escorted out by the local police two days earlier".

"Right," said Bortsov, turning to address the Ambassador. "My guess is that those two people are Americans, probably CIA, and based at the Embassy here. And they would have been able to get some help from the Japanese police, under instructions from their PSIA security service people. I would like to talk to your government contacts if possible and also with the head of the PSIA – I guess you have a contact there, Livitsky?"

"I agree", said the Ambassador. "Let's get on with it while you check into your hotel and we will let you know what can be arranged as soon as possible. The problem here is that the Japanese authorities work very closely with the Americans, of course, but they stay at a polite arms length from us, partly because of that long-running dispute over the Kuril Islands."

Chapter 8

A Missing Person

After the meeting with Bortsov, General Malinov called his deputy, Yevgeny Ivanov, who was the Chief Political Officer at the Embassy and a former member of the Presidential staff in Moscow and said he needed advice. When he arrived in the Ambassador's office, Livitsky was still there and between them, they described the situation concerning the missing naval attache.

"So with your contacts here, Yevgeny, can you help us to prepare several possibilities which we can discuss later with Yuri Bortsov from GRU – he has arrived here today from Moscow to investigate the situation," the General continued. "So far, we have formally notified the foreign affairs department and the local police that Aldanov is a missing person and asking them to make inquiries. We informed them of the details about where he was last seen in the park, but we did not mention the apparent involvement of two police officers. I thought we would save that information until we can see someone senior in the Home Affairs department.

"Then we need to get a meeting with a top man in the PSIA security agency to see if their network of sleuths can dig out any information regarding a missing Russian diplomat and the possible involvement of the CIA. I also want to meet with the minister at the Foreign Affairs department who liaises with all the embassies here. I want to raise two matters formally – firstly their failure to inform us that Aldanov was due to give evidence in court, which would have been a normal courtesy; and secondly to ask them to contact the American Ambassador about their apparent involvement in the incident in which our naval attache was picked up in a vehicle believed to have been from the American Embassy."

"Sounds like quite a challenge," replied Ivanov, thoughtfully stroking his chin. "I am sure that between us we can arrange the meetings you want, but whether we will get any useful replies is doubtful. As usual, we will get lots of bowing, offers of tea and courteous replies with offers to be of assistance – but no actual answers or information. When do we make a start?"

"Now, I think, while Bortsov is resting at his hotel to recover from his flight", said the Ambassador. "I know he will be anxious to have some meetings arranged as soon as possible."

Livitsky was despatched to instruct his team of agents to talk to their usual contacts to see if there were any rumours among their network of contacts about a missing diplomat. And without further delay, the Ambassador and his deputy agreed on who each of them would try to contact and they started to make calls, working separately from both ends of the large office. As expected, the calls were lengthy and slow while efforts were made in each Japanese governmental organisation to find interpreters, or where necessary those with English as a shared language, before they could try to make appointments for such senior level meetings. After using their diplomatic charm to the maximum in spite of the frustrations, they eventually compared notes and found that they had succeeded in fixing a top level meeting in the foreign affairs department later that afternoon and also that Ivanov would be able to meet his PSIA contact for a quiet drink in the evening. And, conveniently, as it happened, the Minister at the Home Affairs department would be unable to meet them until the next morning.

After collecting their thoughts and sharing more details of their phone calls, the Ambassador asked his assistant to call Yuri Bortsov at his hotel. When he came on the line, the General apologised for disturbing him, but when he had described the progress they had made, with the first meeting in just a hour's time, they agreed to leave together in 30 minutes.

The limousine was ready to take the three senior Russians to the Japanese Ministry of Foreign Affairs in Chiyoda City, where they were expected and welcomed by bowing staffers in the reception area and then taken to the third-floor office of Deputy Minister Hashimoto, whose responsibilities included liaison with foreign embassies. He was waiting with two of his staff and they greeted the Russian Ambassador and his deputy, Yevgeny Ivanov, by name as they all bowed appropriately. The Ambassador then politely introduced Bortsov, the GRU chief from Moscow and explained that he had arrived in Tokyo that morning. After further formalities, they were all directed to seats around the large conference table.

"First, I owe you an apology Ambassador," began the minister using perfect English and taking the initiative. "I received your message yesterday regarding our oversight about informing you in advance about the court hearing concerning the unfortunate incident in the Ginza. Apparently, the case had been delayed by the illness of a lawyer, but the justice department then had an opportunity to open the case at short notice and did not advise my department in advance either. But I understand your naval attache gave very satisfactory evidence and they are satisfied at this stage."

"Thank you, Hashimoto-san," replied the Ambassador. "These problems happen, I suppose, but there is a further matter we want to raise with you concerning the same man. His name is Aldanov and he has not been seen since he left his apartment to return to his office as usual the next morning. We have reported him as missing to the police authorities, but we also have a report that he may have been intercepted as he walked through a park on his way to the office by two people, believed to be Americans".

The Japanese minister turned inquiringly to his colleagues who shook their heads to indicate that this was the first they had heard about this, so he smiled and told the Russian trio: "Your man Aldanov seems to be accident prone. He gets shot when he goes to the Ginza and now gets picked up by strangers in a park on his way to the Embassy."

"But there is more," continued the Ambassador. "I am told that he spoke with the two strangers in the park for a few moments

49

and then three of them were approached by two of your uniformed police officers who escorted them into a waiting car nearby which then drove away at high speed".

These further details got the full attention of the Japanese group, who shared worried glances at each other as Ivanov took up the discussion and told the minister firmly: "Since this matter involves your police and possibly the American embassy too, we would like to ask your department to coordinate the inquiry. We assume the two officers were acting on instructions from someone and they must know who was involved in taking Aldanov away? We will share any further information we can get from the person who witnessed the abduction."

"I see," replied Hashimoto, now looking concerned and turning to involve his two staff members who were vigorously writing notes. After talking to them for several minutes in Japanese, he apologised for being discourteous and told the Russian group: "We will start some investigations today and try to throw some light on the mystery – and hopefully find your man. Is there anything else we can do?"

Bortsov then added: "I also plan to talk to my opposite number at the PSIA because as you know, our security services do collaborate from time to time where we have mutual interests. Aldanov is a actually a former secret service agent and he could therefore be useful to another country – not necessarily America, but maybe even Japan?"

Deputy Minister Hashimoto took a deep breath after this final comment and told them: "Thank you gentlemen," indicating the end of the meeting and adding: "I now understand the importance of your problem. We will make some urgent inquiries and inform you of progress tomorrow".

With more bowing and polite farewells, the three Russians were escorted from the office to the lift and back to their car, where Ivanov turned to Bortsov and told him: "That is as good as it gets here. Underneath the formalities, we are not best friends with the Japanese government and they will always look after the interests of the Americans."

"I get the message," said Bortsov. "I think I will see the PSIA man on my own this evening if you don't mind. Shall we reconvene in the Ambassador's office in the morning?"

On their way, the General thanked his two colleagues for their support at the meeting and said that they would meet again at 9am. Bortsov then added with a wry smile: "They were right about accident prone Aldanov ... and they did not even know about the incident in England." As they parted at the Embassy, the Ambassador said he would contact them both if there were any new developments.

Chapter 9

A New Identity

Nikolai Aldanov was deep in thought as he sipped his morning cup of coffee and surveyed the scene from his window – the sun was shining over the treelined roads and the multi-storey buildings of the CIA headquarters in Langley, Virginia. "I wonder what happens next?" he was thinking, as his phone rang….but it was not Alexander as he expected but the head of the Russian section.

"Hi - this is David," came the reassuring voice, adding a good morning greeting in Russian, which Aldanov reciprocated. "Can you be ready in about 30 minutes to join me for breakfast? I will come to collect you". Then adding with a laugh: "Come casual and don't bother to shave. You will be growing a beard soon."

This was a sudden reminder to Aldanov of what was to come. He showered and found that the blue jeans, golf shirt and sneakers provided by Annette fitted perfectly and he was ready when his new American colleague arrived at the door of the building in a large blue saloon car. "I thought I would welcome you with a quick tour of the neighbourhood and an American breakfast," said David as the new arrival climbed into the front seat beside him.

They drove out of the CIA complex into the Parkway and Aldanov was given a commentary about the area as they made their way in the commuter traffic until they reached a parade of shops and pulled into the parking lot and then found the sign for IHOP - the International House of Pancakes. David said he thought this would be something different and a taste of life in the USA – and after they settled down to their plates of pancakes with maple syrup and bacon, plus a large orange juice and coffee, David began to explain to an inquisitive Aldanov what would happen next.

"Your room is in a special high security building which also houses the New Identity Section, where we have a team of experts ready to help you," he began. "This is the last time you will be Nikolai Aldanov and you will be staying in that same building now for the next week or two. We will look after all your needs there and they are a very friendly group, so you will not be lonely. And when you are ready to emerge and meet the rest of our team you will have a new name, new documents, a new appearance and so on. But I imagine that with your past experience with the secret services, you were expecting all this?"

"Yes, I guess so," came a cautious reply. "But it still sounds rather daunting. What will happen after all that … and can I choose my new name?"

"Of course," replied David. "You will be involved in every decision and then the new you, whoever that is, will be introduced into the East European section to begin a training program with some other newcomers. They will have many different backgrounds and in due course, each of you will be assigned to the operational duties most suited to your talents. And you have many."

The conversation became more relaxed as they completed breakfast and took a different route back to Langley so that the Russian could appreciate more of his new environment. This took in a brief view of the Potomac River, the Washington monument and the Capitol building in the distance. Eventually, back at the CIA headquarters, David took the newcomer to the office of the department leader and introduced him to Russell Braddon. He appeared to Nikolai to be younger than expected and rather intense as he explained that this was a **preliminary** meeting to enable him to make a first assessment of his new client, before starting the more detailed work the next day.

David departed and this "preliminary" meeting continued for the rest of the morning, joined by two of Russell's staff who he introduced as Sarah and Tim. It soon became clear that they had already done a great deal of preparation in assembling a new background story together with some sample documentation which they all reviewed. "But first things first," said Russell. "We have to decide on a new name. Any preferences?"

"Would it be easier if I stuck with Nick as a first name?" came the reply.

"Maybe," replied Russell, thoughtfully. "It is okay as a name here too, of course. But I think we need to put as much distance as possible between your new personality and the old one. Also, we need to realise that although you speak quite good English, you have an accent which can be easily recognised as East European, if not Russian. So your background story may need to be Polish, or maybe Ukrainian."

"Yes", said Tim, joining into the process. "We had in mind a name like Welensky, with a back story which includes an immigrant family and parentage but perhaps being born in New York. Then we need an American first name, something like Louis or Lou for short, or maybe Henry or Hank? What do you think?"

After a thoughtful pause came the reply: "OK – I can live with Lou Welensky if you think that will work".

"Right – so welcome to the CIA, Lou," said Russell, standing up as they all shook hands warmly. "And let's get to work".

He then went on to explain in detail how their objective was to replace everything in his memory from the past 30-plus years with a completely new personality. Over the coming days and weeks, he would become so accustomed to being Lou that he would not even know when they were actually testing him. Meanwhile, he continued, they would be working on his physical appearance and later on, take a new photograph for an American passport, plus all the other documentation he would need.

The Russian listened carefully, nodding his agreement from time to time, until Russell ended by telling him what he had been expecting: "But first, before you forget your past life, you will be having some sessions starting tomorrow with a couple of our specialists to gather all the information you can recall about your time in GRU – all the names, locations, operations, systems and so on. You will meet them tomorrow from about 9am, so you have some time to start thinking about it and making a few notes. Also, I will leave you with Sarah to help prepare your American paperwork and to start working out everything you will need to feel at home here as Lou Welensky. Do you have any questions at this stage?"

"Thank you, but no – you seem to have thought of everything," came the confident reply..

Chapter 10

Searching for Evidence

In Tokyo, Yuri Bortsov of the GRU went to his prearranged rendezvous in the spacious lounge bar of the Okura Hotel with Akio Watanabe, the Deputy Director of Japan's security and intelligence service, the PSIA. Although they had not previously met, they had each done some rapid research about the other and their observation skills ensured that they soon recognised each other. They shook hands warmly and found a quiet corner to relax and order two brandies.

"That's a surprise, Watanabe-san," said Bortsov, speaking slowly in English as the waiter went to get their drinks. "I thought it would be saki and vodka." They relaxed with a laugh, which was a good start to their meeting and the Japanese official added: "I admire the work of your department and we are both men of the world. Sorry not to understand Russian, but I speak good English and enjoy brandy".

When the drinks arrived, they toasted each other, and Hashimoto said: It is always a pleasure to welcome a colleague from another country. So what is the problem? You obviously have something on your mind as well as sharing a brandy with me."

"Have you heard about our missing diplomat?" came the response, and after getting a negative reply and a shake of the head, Bortsov decided to describe the entire sequence of events from the shooting incident in the Ginza and the court hearing to the discussion in the taxi with his GRU agent and the incident the next day in the park. And he ended: "The missing man is Nikolai Aldanov, he is the naval attache at our embassy here and he previously served with the GRU in Moscow. So we are very concerned."

"Ah yes, of course - I knew about the shooting and the attempted murder trial, of course," said Watanabe. "And I know that another man from your embassy was also shot and is still in hospital. So we have all been monitoring his condition carefully in case he fails to recover, which of course would make it a very different matter. I am glad your man recovered to give evidence this week, but I had not heard about what happened to him afterwards. How can we be of assistance to you?"

"I am concerned about the involvement of two of your police officers in the incident in the park and by the suspicion that the people he met and disappeared with were Americans," continued Bortsov. "I am hoping that your network may be able to discover some further facts about the two policemen. Who had given them their instructions? Also, is there any information or rumours among your people about American involvement – such as who might be holding Aldanov and where?"

"Yes, I can see now why you are so concerned," said Watanabe, pausing for a few moments before adding: "I am thinking about how we can help. Obviously, you are not able to question the policemen directly, or discover anything from the American embassy. I do not imagine you are on good terms with the CIA people there, but my people have some useful contacts. Let me get back to you tomorrow."

As they shared their contact numbers, Bortsov added that the Russian Ambassador had set up a meeting for the next morning with an official at the Home Affairs department, specifically to ask about the apparent involvement of the Tokyo police officers. Watanabe said he was glad to know about that planned meeting, which would help him avoid crossing lines and they shook hands and went their separate ways.

The next morning, Bortsov and Livitsky met with the Ambassador and his deputy Yevgeny Ivanov, the Chief Political Officer, but they had no further developments to share other than the news that the PSIA chief had agreed to use their network to seek out any information about the missing Russian attache. But the Ambassador said he was not too hopeful – "The Japanese will want to keep their noses clean so far as the Americans are concerned."

The group then set off in the Ambassador's limousine for the Japanese Home Office for the appointment with a Deputy Director who was known to Ivanov and introduced himself to the group as Tanaka-san. He was accompanied by four other members of his staff and there was much bowing before they all settled down at a large conference table. Eventually, the Ambassador was able to explain why they were there, describing how his naval attache, Nikolai Aldanov, had disappeared two days earlier after giving evidence in the court hearing about the shooting incident in the Ginza. At this, the Japanese group all nodded and muttered words indicating that they knew all about the shooting.

Then Ivanov took over and said: "Tanaka-san, the problem is that when Aldanov left his apartment the next day to walk to the Russian embassy, he stopped to talk to two people and then two Japanese policemen in uniform were seen to escort the group to a waiting car which drove off at great speed. We have not heard from our man since, so we are very concerned. We would like to know who gave your police officers their instructions and what do they know about the other two people who met Aldanov and also details about the car? We can show you the exact location so maybe you can also check any CCTV coverage of the area at the time in question and then allow us to see the results, please? We need to identify the people involved."

Tanaka nodded his understanding of the information and the questions, and the four members of the Home Office staff had been busily writing notes while the Ambassador and his deputy described the problem. He then turned to one of them and gave some instructions which the Russians did not understand and all four of them stood up, bowed again and left the room. The deputy minister then told his visitors that he had ordered coffee for them all and also that one of his team would be making immediate contact with the police department. "I am sure he will come back with some information for you shortly," he added.

Coffee arrived quickly and the group tactfully discussed other matters including the weather and how much of Japan the Russians had been able to visit. Eventually, one of the aides returned and whispered quietly into Tanaka's ear. The official nodded frequently as he listened and then turned to the

Ambassador and his colleagues: "I am sorry to keep you so long, but the police chief for the area has no knowledge of the incident and will take a few hours to discover which officers were on duty in that park at the time you described. He will also discover the locations of any relevant CCTV cameras. Who should I contact when I get any further details?"

They agreed that he should respond to Ivanov – and the group showed their disappointment as they took their leave and returned to their car, where the Ambassador slumped into his seat and said to his colleagues firmly: "I told you so. It is what I expected, probably because their inquiries revealed that the Americans are involved."

"I get the picture," said Bortsov. "Let me see what the PSIA man can discover from his contacts and meanwhile we must start thinking about where the Americans could be hiding Aldanov."

Back at the embassy, he was pleased to find a message from Akio Watanabe, his counterpart in the Japanese intelligence agency, to call as soon as possible. They quickly arranged another rendezvous at the Okura hotel and he was already there at a quiet corner with two brandies on the table when Bortsov arrived.

"I have some news," he began. "My team have tracked a CCTV camera near the point where your man had his rendezvous. It is quite distant, but they can see three people getting into the vehicle and as it drives off, they are able recognise it as a known US embassy limo. But they can find no evidence of two of our police officers being in the area and we suspect that the whole thing was an elaborate American set-up."

"That's a good start," said Bortsov, welcoming the information and congratulating the Japanese investigators on their fast action. "So what next?"

"Well, we strongly disapprove of a foreign power apparently impersonating our uniformed police officers," continued Watanabe. "And we also think that this Russian may have been kidnapped, so we will be taking this matter formally to the American Ambassador for an explanation and we will keep you informed, of course."

"So where would they be hiding Aldanov? Or could he have left the country by now?" asked Bortsov.

"We have started checking the airports," said Watanabe. "And we also know of several American safe houses in Tokyo and elsewhere as well as the various US military establishments of course, so it could be like searching for a needle in a haystack – unless one of our agents can get a tip-off from a contact? I assure you that they are working on it."

"Good work, Watanabe-san," said Bortsov, as they decided to stay in touch and went their separate ways.

Chapter 11

The De-briefing

It was Lou Welensky's second day in the comfortable and modern residential suite of the New Identity Section at the CIA headquarters in Langley, Virginia. In the bathroom, he stroked his bristled chin and remembered the advice not to have his usual shave. The, in the small kitchen, he found some of his favourite cereals and fruit, made coffee and then surveyed the selection of more casual American clothes which had been delivered by Sarah during the previous evening. He chose a colourful T-shirt and light jacket and hoped it was right for the occasion ahead that morning. He was watching the TV news when his phone rang and it was David who asked him to go down to the ground floor meeting room when he was ready.

He found David there, seated at the conference table with two older and more formally dressed men who were introduced as Wilbur and James from the East European research section. They stood and welcomed him warmly and told him to relax because they had a long day ahead. They took off their jackets and loosened their neckties as David began to explain the next stage in Lou's programme.

"I don't need to tell you how important it is for us to find someone with your background ready to work with us," he began. "You may have seen it happen from the other side, of course."

"Not exactly," said Lou. "But I have heard about these de-briefings and I know what to expect."

"That sounds good," said David, as he prepared to leave the new arrival with his interrogators. "I will be back later to see how it is going."

Wilbur then took the initiative and began by explaining that they would take their time and make it as easy for Lou as possible. He said that he and James had both been with the CIA for many years, they had served overseas and in particular had worked in the embassies in Moscow, Warsaw and other countries in Europe. "We both had spells in the field as operatives in our younger days, before becoming analysts," he explained. "When we start, we will be recording our conversations, by the way, but it will all be scrambled before it goes into the archives, so anything you can help us with will remain completely confidential."

Lou nodded his agreement and understanding, and James then began by asking about his educational years, his decision to join the Russian Navy and the reason for deciding to then retire from the service to apply for a new career in Government with the Defence ministry. In his replies, Lou was careful to not use his real name and, with occasional promptings from his interrogator, he described every stage in as much detail as he could recall.

The atmosphere was relaxed and they paused from time to time to pour cups of coffee from the machine and water from the jugs until they reached the stage where their interviewee began to describe his formal training as a secret service agent with the GRU. "Let's take a break now so that you can collect your thoughts with a stroll outside in the sunshine and then maybe some lunch," said Wilbur, pressing the buzzer to attract Sarah from the adjoining office.

When they returned after about 15 minutes walking along the pathways around the Agency campus, the requested sandwiches and sodas had arrived and when the plates and glasses were cleared away, Lou was ready for the next question: "So what was your first impression of the GRU section you joined?"

"They were all so serious and intense – not a bit like the Navy," he began. "The working hours were long and the senior officer responsible for my training period gave me a combination of reading material and then questions to be sure I had understood the documents. They were mainly reports describing in great detail some of the operations the section had been involved with in recent years."

Lou was encouraged to recall as much detail as he could and he was interrupted each time he mentioned one of the individuals working on the missions. "In particular", said Wilbur, breaking his silence, "We would like to build a file of as many names as you can remember – those at the HQ and those working overseas and the locations where they were based."

The questions and answers continued through the rest of the day and the two CIA analysts seemed to be pleased with the results from their hours of questioning when David returned to ask how it was going?

"I am sure you are ready for a relaxing evening, Lou," he said. "We would like you to stay here in this unit for a day or two more and Sarah will find out what to order you for an evening meal. I will see you again in the morning to tell you what happens next."

Lou was feeling tired and gratefully returned to his upstairs suite to relax. David wished him a good rest and as he and his two colleagues walked back towards the main office block, he asked: "So what do you make of him?"

"Very interesting," replied Wilbur, thoughtfully. "He is very bright, a bit impetuous I suspect and obviously very anxious to be helpful. He said several times that he is hoping to be able to work as an agent again, this time for us. But I am not sure yet how much he really knows about the workings of the GRU – he was not there many months before he went off on his ill-fated venture to Britain. I think we need another session tomorrow to dig a bit deeper and test the validity of some of the things he is telling us".

And James agreed, adding: "I suggest we have Henri with us tomorrow – he has the most recent experience of working in our Moscow embassy and he will know what they were able to monitor about GRU activities."

Chapter 12

Covering Up?

Yuri Bortsov, Director of the GRU, Russia's secret service, was uncharacteristically showing his anger. He was again in the Tokyo office of the Russian Ambassador to Japan for another early morning meeting to hear that the Japanese government had not taken any serious action regarding the missing diplomat.

Ambassador Malinov had just read to him the message received a few minutes earlier from his contact at the Home Affairs department: "Further to your meeting with Minister Tanaka yesterday, we have instituted enquiries with the departments concerned but have no additional information to assist you at this stage," read the formal document. It continued: "We will inform you if there are any new developments from our inquiries and I hope you are successful in finding your naval attache and that he is fit and well."

"That seems typical," said Bortsov, shaking his head in disbelief. "But taken with the comments from my PSIA contact yesterday, it seems to me that they are covering up for the Americans. I think this has the hallmark of a CIA operation and that Aldanov is now holed up in the US embassy while they grill him for what he knows."

The Ambassador agreed and the two Russians went on to review carefully all the information to date one more time to be sure they had not missed anything important. Bortsov said he intended to fly back to Moscow later the same day and would continue to coordinate the search from head office. He sent a message to his confidential number for Watanabe, his contact at the PSIA, asking him to call when convenient. Then another call was made to the administration office to book a suitable return flight later in the day and then they decided to call Pavel Livitsky to join them for a final review.

"I am leaving this in your good hands and will be flying back to Moscow today", Bortsov told his local GRU bureau chief. "But I want you and your team to stay focussed on the disappearance of Aldnanov as top priority. Can you all keep your ears to the ground in your usual network to see if there are any clues about the involvement of the CIA. We suspect that he is either hidden away in the American embassy or at one of the secure military bases. Or perhaps they have even flown him out from Japan already. My contact at PSIA is checking on flight departures but there is also the possibility that they used one of the US air force bases here– and I understand that there are no travel formalities for those arriving and leaving on military aircraft".

The group continued to speculate as they were served with coffee, and came to the conclusion that it had been a well-planned CIA operation and that the vehicle might not have even returned to the American embassy, but had driven directly to a waiting aircraft at a US base. They also considered whether the two police officers might have been locally-based characters hired by the CIA for the occasion? This led the Ambassador to the conclusion that the incident might not be a matter for the

Japanese authorities after all, but a direct confrontation between the US and Russian governments about the apparent abduction of a Russian diplomat. They were mulling over this thought when Bortsov's phone trilled its indication of a confidential call. It was his Japanese secret service contact.

"Hello Watanabe-san and thanks for returning my call", he began. "I just needed to tell you that I have decided to fly back to Moscow later today and continue to lead the enquiries from there. Do you have any updates for me before I go?"

"No, there is nothing new," came the cautious reply. "But it was good to meet you and I hope we can stay in touch and that you find your man safely somewhere."

"Can I give your direct number to Livitsky? He's my bureau chief here, and he can then continue to liaise with you on this matter?" asked Bortsov.

And Watanabe quickly responded: "If I did that, I would have to change my number – so I am sorry and if anything else occurs which would be helpful, I will know where to find your man or I can get a message to you. So have a good flight." And the call ended abruptly.

Bortsov turned to the others, shaking his head and sharing the brief conversation. "As you said earlier, General, we are not favourites with the Japanese and this seems to confirm to me that their secret service people are working with the Americans on this matter."

The Ambassador confirmed that this was his usual experience in all the official contacts he made with the Japanese foreign affairs staff – "We just have to get used to it, I'm afraid," he added, philosophically. There was no time for more discussion as his assistant arrived in the office with the flight details for their visitor and confirmation that a car was waiting outside to take him to the airport.

As he prepared to leave, Bortsov told them: "One more thing before I go. I was quite taken with your man Ilia – he is very bright, looks younger than he really is and he has a quiet personality. These are just the qualities I need in our Special Operations team. When I get back, I plan to start the process of moving him back to Moscow and I will work on sending you a replacement. Okay?"

There were rapid farewells between the group and the spy chief was clearly not in the mood to say more – leaving the Ambassador and his colleague to contemplate on what to do next?

Chapter 13

The CIA's Verdict

Lou Welensky looked into a mirror and thought his new beard looked promising. After two weeks without shaving, it was beginning to alter his appearance – and he quite liked it. Meanwhile, Russell Braddon and his team had done their work, aided by a hairdresser to create a new short style, plus some fashionable, though unnecessary, spectacles. They also briefed him repeatedly on his new back story – his upbringing in New York, his family and his early career including a spell at sea as a trainee officer in the merchant navy as a way of utilising his existing maritime knowledge.

All this, together with further intensive debriefing sessions with Wilbur and James combined to help Lou become acclimatised to his new life. But he was severely tested when their colleague Henri joined the interrogation and revealed that he had spent two years with the intelligence gathering unit at the US Embassy in Moscow. He clearly knew more than enough about the GRU activities and personel at the Diamond to ask some searching questions.

"I have seen the notes prepared by James from their sessions with you," Henri began. "You described the team you were working with in your time there pretty well and also some of the operations. But there are a few gaps you might be able to recall if I reminded you."

He then described a series of operational activities which were taking place in GRU at the relevant time and Lou was surprised to discover just how much the Americans knew. He was able to add a few names and locations which seemed to satisfy Henri and he went on to explain that he was mainly working as an analyst at that time. This was a desk job reviewing the reports from their teams in other countries, so he was only on the fringe of the other activities.

"So how did you find time to start up an on-line relationship with an English woman," asked Henri.

"I am sure you know that my wife was sick at the time," explained Lou. "I had left the Navy for a government job to be with her and after she sadly died, I had time to fill and it was my ambition to get promotion and to work as an agent in the field. So I was looking for ways to impress my boss and show some initiative and I came up with this idea of trying to find useful informants on these dating websites. I could hardly believe my luck when after several weeks of searching in my spare time, I discovered this woman who worked for the British navy."

"OK, I know the rest of the story," Henri interrupted. "But it didn't work out well for you or for your boss who approved your adventure. But thanks for sharing your memories with us".

At the end of Lou's second week, David Boronovich, the head of the CIA Russian section had a debriefing meeting with Russell

Braddon and Wilbur Smith – "So what is your verdict on our new man?" he asked.

"I think he is going to be ok," replied Russell, rather cautiously. "He seems a bit over-confident for a new boy, but I guess he has packed quite a lot into his life, and he cannot change his entire personality now. His over-riding ambition is still to become an operational agent. That is what is driving him, and I think the field training period may teach us a lot more about his potential."

Wilbur Smith concurred and agreed that they had not discovered any serious concerns. David said he agreed and concluded the session: "Then I think it is time to let him out of purdah and get him out on to the field training stage. This usually sorts out the men from the boys. I will give him a briefing on Monday morning, and he can join the programme that starts in the middle of next week".

He then asked Russell to arrange for Lou to move out from the closed induction area after nearly three weeks and into the nearby training section of the CIA campus and one of the small single apartments there used by new recruits. There was also a recreation room, a gymnasium and a pool and it was just a short walk from the staff dining area. He soon discovered that his new neighbours were anxious to welcome him when he arrived with his personal belongings. During weekend introductions, he realised that his fellow trainees were mostly younger, but they had all learned the agency code of discretion in their conversations. He also soon discovered that he needed to learn much more about baseball, rap music and the American TV soaps.

As he settled into this new phase in his life, relaxing as much as possible with the books and TV in his room, he became apprehensive when he received a message from David. It told him that he would be collected on Monday morning at 8.45 to go to a meeting with the Deputy Director, Bob Smithers in the HQ building at 9am. This would be the first time they had met since he had shared a brief but cordial conversation during the long flight from Tokyo more than four weeks earlier in the chief 's luxurious Learjet.

It seemed like a lifetime ago.

Chapter 14

A Plan for Revenge

It was a ten-hours Aeroflot flight from Tokyo back to Moscow which gave Yuri Bortsov plenty of time to ponder the situation he had left behind, together with the wider tasks he had been set to reverse the image of his new department. On his mind were the words he had heard at that important meeting a week earlier when the Minister in charge of security and the GRU secret service told him sternly: "It is not a good scene and we need to take action."

His boss had gone on to describe his anger about the "Aldanov fiasco" in Portsmouth, followed now by the strange disappearance of the same man in Japan, possibly into the hands of the CIA. Then there was the diplomat from the embassy in London who was now in prison as well as another failed incident in England when two agents had been arrested and jailed after hitting the wrong target with their Ricin gun. He was also concerned about the mysterious new CIA woman who seemed to be involved in some way with the recent setbacks they had experienced in Canada and now Japan.

As Bortsov settled into the comfort of his first-class seat, he ordered a vodka from the attractive Russian flight attendant and exchanged a few pleasantries with the Japanese passenger in the adjoining seat. In their few mutual words of English, he discovered that his neighbour was an executive with a company importing vodka from a supplier in Moscow. So satisfied that they had little in common, he began to analyse the recent events in his department.

He took his electronic tablet from his briefcase, found that he could get a wifi signal and using his password system, he signed on to his confidential messages. First, his assistant had forwarded an important update from Livitsky, his bureau chief In Tokyo. He had discovered from his secret mole in the US embassy that a Russian man had in fact been brought into the building a few days earlier but had then been driven away early in the following morning.

"Good work," was Bortsov's succinct response in reply.

Using his tablet, he started to prepare an outline of his future challenges and some possible solutions. He decided that challenge number one was tracking down Aldanov, who he could now assume to be somewhere in the hands of the CIA. This had been in his thoughts when he made the decision earlier that day to move the young agent Pavel Ilia to Moscow. Ilia had been the last person to talk to Aldanov before his disappearance and he could be a vital part of the investigation – either in London or the USA? So his next message was to his deputy setting out his instructions to arrange for Pavel Ilia to be transferred from the Tokyo-based GRU team to join the Special Operations group in Moscow.

He then began to draft an outline plan for Ilia to join in a long-term search to discover the whereabouts of Aldanov, initially focussing on London or Washington. The plan went on to identify the possible ways in which the CIA or MI6 could exploit the experiences and knowledge possessed by the former GRU agent and ways to nullify this information – and ultimately to explore ways to eliminate him as a traitor.

Next, Bortsov considered ways in which he would set his experts the task of identifying the troublesome but unknown female CIA agent. The file compiled by his departmental analysts on her activities had tracked her involvement in anti-Russian operations in Canada and then in Tokyo, but it was short of detail on her background and identity. And was she the same woman who was seen with Aldanov when he was picked up in the park?

Next, he decided that he would work with his colleagues in London and Washington to identify a senior British or American official who could be detained while on travel and then held as a hostage to negotiate the release of the Russian diplomat Rozovsky now in jail in London. His experiences could be valuable in developing a response to the embarrassing incident in the UK.

And finally, he would start planning for a major hit on a US military base, probably in the UK, to demonstrate the capabilities of the GRU to strike back after the setbacks of the past year or two.

It was all sounding good as he prepared the first draft of this confidential memorandum, setting out the next stages of his future operations. He decided that he would complete the final version as soon as he returned to his office in Moscow and would then forward it to the defence minister for approval. He began to relax, ordered another vodka and then dinner was served, after which he fell into a deep sleep for several hours until he was woken by the activity around him and the serving of breakfast. There was just an hour's flight time remaining before the arrival into Moscow – where an official limousine would be waiting at the end of a brief but eventful journey.

Chapter 15

"A Great Start"

Lou was ready when David arrived promptly on Monday morning to accompany him on the walk to the main building for the scheduled meeting with the Deputy Chief of Operations, Bob Smithers. When they arrived, they found that Russell Braddon, head of the New Identity section, was already there – following on from his briefing with the boss on the work his department had completed on the new arrival.

"Hey, who's this guy," said Bob Smithers with a laugh as "Lou" entered his office, getting up from his desk and stretching out a hand of welcome. "I don't think I would recognise you. Hey, you've done a terrific job, Russell", he added turning to his identity expert.

They all sat at the conference table and the chief started their meeting by welcoming Lou and telling him: "You've made a great start with us here and I gather the debriefing sessions were very productive. So this is the time to hand over your official documentation."

This was the cue for Russell Braddon to open a folder to explain each item as he passed it over to the newcomer. There was a American passport, a mobile phone, two credit cards and several documents which Lou was asked to sign with his new signature. It was explained that these documents would confirm his new assignment to the CIA as an "operative in training". The others then stood as Bob Smithers rose to his feet and with a formal handshake, welcomed Louis Welensky … "as an American citizen and a member of The Company". He wished him success and added: "I will be getting regular reports on how you are settling in with us. I know it will not be easy, but David will be your first point of contact if you have any problems, and you will continue to live here on base until the training stage is completed. Any questions so far?"

A rather bewildered newcomer tried hard to compose himself and managed to say he had no questions before Smithers continued: "Right, now let's talk about what happens next."

He went on to describe the objectives of training programme which lay ahead which he said would start the next day and which occupied most of his time and energy over the weeks that followed.

Lou discovered the next day that there were three other new CIA recruits in the small group which he joined for a demanding schedule which ranged from talks on organization and procedures in the Company to field training and gun handling. The others were in their early 30s, who had been recruited from less demanding careers – two of them, Greg and Robert, had joined from other US government departments and the fourth was Alexa with a Filipino family background. She had been recruited after serving in the US military police for five years and was looking for a career change "with a bit more action".

The programme began with an all-day communications briefing, which proved to be one of the more demanding sessions. The new recruits were taken to a securely guarded wing of the main building and in a windowless room where they were each issued with the latest CIA smartphone followed by instructions on its range of new functions. These included how to switch it from normal usage into a secure network with end-to-end encryption. They were impressed to learn that these phones could also be used to track their locations when working in the field. Then there was a confidential CIA number which required special codes and passwords to be used – and memorised.

Lou was relieved to find that his two fellow recruits from Government backgrounds took the initiative with searching questions, and they all became even more impressed when the cyber-security expert went on to describe the methods used by the Agency to handle secret information. These included the use of hidden microphones and minicameras as well as laptop computers which needed to be authenticated with passwords that changed every hour. They were also introduced to a new generation of phones which opened with biometric information such as fingerprints and facial recognition.

The newcomer quickly recognised that these developments were more sophisticated that anything he had seen in his previous career, especially when the presenter went on to tell them: "Just bear in mind that it is not just in the movies that you can see fly-on-the-wall micro-drones which can be remote-controlled, even inside a building to transmit encrypted recordings of what is happening there. And there really are spy cameras in satellites which can read the number plate on a car.

So there is always new miniaturised technology and applications being tested by our team and then used by you guys in the field."

This session certainly got their full attention and all the group, including Lou, had questions which kept the session going until late in the afternoon. At the end they were in no doubt about the work going on behind the scenes to provide the tools of espionage, security and counter-intelligence operations. It certainly opened the eyes of the group into the unseen skills of those working behind the scenes in the Company.

Then next day, there was another intensive all-day classroom session, this time on international politics and ideologies. And for their final classroom day, they were treated to lengthy briefings and discussions with serving agents on their recent and current experiences. This included detailed blow-by-blow descriptions – including videos - of some hair-raising exploits which left them in no doubt about the future which faced them.

These parts of the programme were conducted within the Langley complex, but next there were several days away from the base at a nearby military establishment and a training area in Virginia. For these, they were all issued with military-style overalls and boots for the outdoor activities during which they flew in helicopters, fired weapons, rode in armoured vehicles over rough terrain and tackled a demanding assault course. It was hard going for Greg and Robert who thought they had kept fit with daily jogging in a Washington park and Lou not to show that he found it much harder than he expected. It was Alexa who impressed and encouraged the others throughout the testing programme. She admitted that she had done much of it before in her military training and they had to accept that she was the fittest member of the group.

During their rest periods, the group chatted to their trainers – who had seen it all before and reassured them that they had actually done better than most trainees on the course. And in the evenings back at headquarters, they shared their reactions to the mental and physical demands of the training and got to know each other better. But Lou was cautious and careful to stay with his agreed "back story" as they all enjoyed comparing the different form of English words used by the Filipino Alexa and the Ukrainian Lou.

As the programme reached the end of its final day, they had an informal meeting with the Deputy Director of Operations, Bob Smithers, who reassured them that they were all 'making the grade'. He also surprised them with the news that for a complete change, the next stage would be at another CIA base in Florida for a week of foreign language training. He explained that they would be learning enough Spanish, French and Russian to be useful in emergencies – "enough to get you out of trouble when you get to other countries," he explained.

Lou had already told his colleagues about his Ukrainian family background and his knowledge of Russian, so during their weekend flight to Florida, they enjoyed learning a few words in advance. At Orlando airport they were met by a driver with a US Government sign and a waiting people-carrier to take them to their destination. But first, they were confronted by the barrage of banners and billboards welcoming them the world of Disney – which the Americans enjoyed explaining to Lou as they were eventually driven through more rural and agricultural

Florida until they reached the entrance to Camp Orchard, the CIA's language training centre. It was a more relaxed week and the group had time to enjoy the Florida weather and a trip to the beach on the Gulf coast. But it all came to an end too soon.

Back in Virginia, David met them in the training area with the news that they would now have a few days leave to decide where they planned to live and explained that the administrative office could give them suggestions on where they might find convenient apartments – unless they already had other plans. He added that they could remain in the training section for a few more days while they sorted out their needs. He went on to tell them that their first month's pay was already in their bank accounts, and he also gave them information about the Company scheme to help newcomers with the cost of setting up home with a low interest loan.

"So good luck and well done," he ended. "See you here on the first of the month when you will all hear about your next assignments."

As they relaxed together at last, drinking Cokes in their recreation area, they began to exchange thoughts on what happens next? The other three appeared to already have friends in the nearby Washington suburbs who would accommodate them for a while until their future positions became clear. But not surprisingly, Lou was on his own and he was relieved when Alexa offered to show him round the area the next day.

He gladly accepted – and although he had appreciated during their time together that she was a very attractive and mature Asian lady, he also decided that night that the last thing he needed was another *femme fatale.*

Chapter 16

Plan Approved

Yuri Bortsov returned to his office at GRU headquarters after a good night's sleep in his Moscow apartment to recover from his too-brief but eventful visit to Tokyo. He asked his assistant to print out the report and plan he had prepared during his return flight and send it immediately to the minister in the defence department with a request for a meeting. He did not have to wait long before the call came.

General Yazov, the Deputy Minister was waiting to greet Bortsov with a handshake and congratulations. "I think the Tokyo air has been good for you," he said. "Your plan looks very much on target to me and I am confident that you can turn things around."

They went through the details, point by point, and not surprisingly he focussed on the proposal to plan a major strike on a US military base, probably in the UK, to demonstrate the capabilities of the GRU to strike back. "Take a careful look at two or three possible targets and keep me informed at each step in your planning," he concluded, and he wished his GRU chief success.

There was a spring in Bortsov's step as he walked back from the minister's office to the car waiting to whisk him back to The Diamond. And there, he wasted no time in calling a meeting with the director of his Special Operations section, Dimitri Kotov, who had many years of field experience with the GRU and KGB before that. He also asked him to bring one of the younger agents in the section called Egerov, who had already impressed him during his first weeks in the job. His record showed previous overseas experience, notably with the secret services team in London.

They gathered in the Director's specially-designed conference room adjoining his office. It was fitted with double-layer silicone security protection against any form of external listening device which could be directed at the building. None of them had been in the room previously and Bortsov explained that it was a necessary protection – "in case the enemy's listening systems are as good as ours!".

He then greeted each of them warmly and began: "You are here because we have a very important and challenging time ahead of us. I have prepared a plan of action which is intended to restore the reputation of the GRU with our bosses in the Kremlin. As you all know, we have taken a few hits lately and my plans have been approved today by Minister Yazov and you are my special team to carry it out during the next few weeks. And I do not need to tell you that this is even more confidential than anything else."

This got their attention, and Kotov even more so when his boss continued: "Our first challenge is to find Nikolai Aldanov who I believe has been abducted by the American CIA – and of course both of you will remember him from his previous time here in our analyst team."

"Yes, indeed" came the immediate reply from Kotov. "He was not in my section, of course, but we were all mystified by what happened to him. He seemed to be a pretty bright guy, but he was kicked out after a failed mission in London, as I recall."

Kotov continued to describe how he knew about Aldanov's ambition to become an agent and he had persuaded the previous Director to allow him to pursue an opportunity he had created through an on-line dating website to find a new potential informant in the British navy.

"As you know," continued Kotov, "The Director lost his job over the incident and that was when you arrived. In case you don't know all the details, Aldanov was assigned to join one of our ships which was due to visit Britain but it all went wrong when he became infatuated with this woman and quite stupidly did not realise that his on-line messages were being monitored by British intelligence. So it was not surprising when we heard he had been arrested at the woman's apartment. After that, things went haywire when our London people tried to limit the damage by sending agents to try to silence the woman before she could give damaging evidence at Aldanov's trial.

"The next thing was a great deal of negative press coverage about the man they called the Russian Lieutenant, and it got even worse. The woman was poisoned by our agents and at her funeral, our naval attache at the embassy got involved and was arrested as an accomplice to her murder and he is still in a British jail. But Aldanov came back to Moscow in a spy-swap and he was sacked from the GRU and sent to a quiet job at the embassy in

Japan. And as you know, he was then injured in a shooting incident with two anti-Russian protesters. But he was not as badly injured as his colleague from the embassy who is still in hospital."

Bortsov said he was pleased to hear more details of the story and then surprised them both with the latest development as he described the apparent abduction of Aldanov by the CIA in Tokyo. Then he turned to Kotov and told him that there would be one more new member to his team to work on this matter – he was Pavel Ilia, who was the last person at the embassy in Tokyo to talk to Aldanov and he was due to return to Moscow in a few days.

He explained: "My assumption is that the CIA had targeted Aldanov as a weak link – but they probably over-estimated his value as an informant. I believe they quickly flew him out of Japan, probably to London or the USA. So our first task, Kotov, is to work with our people in the UK and Washington see if there is any inside information about a Russian arriving there recently. Then if we have a suspect, we will use the new man Ilia to follow the trail to get confirmation of his identity – which may of course have been changed. And then we will arrange his elimination as a traitor. Okay?"

The young Egerov was startled by this at first but said he understood and added: "You may not know that I was actually based in London during those incidents involving Aldanov."

"That's why you are here," replied Bortsov, who then said he would move on to the second part of his operational plan. "This is to try to identify a new CIA woman agent who seems to specialise in Russian targets", he began. "We believe she was involved in the Aldanov abduction in Tokyo and is probably the same one who was identified by our team here as the unknown agent in the raid on the cyber monitoring base in Canada last year. On this one, Kotov, I suggest you start with Livitsky in Tokyo to see if their trail can produce any clues, such as DNA or photos."

There were no questions to raise at this stage and Bortzov sent for coffee to be provided as he warned them that there were two more challenges still to come.

When they were ready and settled again, he continued: "Challenge number three is a bit less specific and Egerov will go back to London to work on this. We want to negotiate for the release of Yakov Rozovsky, the diplomat who is in an English jail. He is a key Kremlin man and they want us to find a suitable hostage for an exchange. There maybe someone here in Moscow, which I will work on. But also can you start working with our people in London to identify a suitably senior official who is on foreign travel and can be picked up on some pretext and detained. This may take some time, of course, but I am sure you know what we are looking for."

His key colleagues said they understood because this was a familiar exercise. But they were then alerted again when Bortsov said: "Now for number four, the big one."

He then described how the top brass in the Defence ministry were looking for a major GRU operation to demonstrate their capabilities – something that would hit the world headlines as a show of Russian power. There were no specifics which he could share at the moment, but they were considering a possible attack on a key target, such as one of the American air bases in the UK or possibly a naval base.

Turning to the two young agents, he added: "There are many possibilities so I am sharing this objective with you now so that in your travels in the next few weeks, you can think about it and make some very discrete inquiries. So if you come up with an idea which fits the bill, share it with me and we will then do a detailed study with our logistics people. Okay?"

The more experienced Kotov had listened intently to the plans outlined by his new director, but decided now to intervene and asked cautiously: "Isn't this more like a project for the military planners than for us in GRU?"

"No, no" came the quick reply. "This has to be a highly secret operation and you well know that with proper preparation, one or two experienced operatives can deliver a major blow to a key installation – maybe a single rocket or even a cyber hit".

Bortsov returned to his four-point plan and began to describe more details. He said he intended to involve the Ambassadors in London and Washington on the first three challenges, as well as the heads of the GRU missions in both embassies. He also planned for Kotov to go to Washington and Egerov to London, plus the new man Ilia to whichever country was most likely to be the target for finding Aldanov.

"I know we have some good sleepers in both places and a network of informants," he explained. "At this stage, we will only tell our people that they should be looking for any clues or rumours about a Russian man who has unexpectedly arrived there, probably with the CIA. If he is there, we can be sure that it will soon be on the grapevine somewhere."

He added that in his conversations with London and Washington, he would also alert their senior overseas colleagues about the need to identify a suitable high profile hostage for a swap with the jailed Russian diplomat in London. And as the meeting ended, Bortsov told them: "I want you to give these challenges our priority and let me know if you come up with new ideas. We will all get together again for an update when we are joined by Ilia from Tokyo."

Chapter 17

The US or the UK?

At the elegant Russian Embassy in London's select and gated Kensington Park area, the diplomat who headed the GRU team was Igor Malenkov, a former colleague of Yuri Bortsov at the Defence Ministry in Moscow. He was delighted to hear that his old friend was on the line and began the conversation by complimenting him on his important new job as Director of GRU.

Bortsov thanked him and then checked whether they were on a secure connection, as he had requested. Getting a positive confirmation, he introduced Kotov and explained that they would be seeking help from the London-based group on two highly confidential inquiries.

"What I can share with you now," he continued, "Is that one of our people has been abducted in Japan and my suspicion is that the CIA are responsible. He may have been flown out to either London or Washington, but I know nothing more than that. I know you have a good team there and a network of informers so what I am asking at this stage is for you and your people to check all your sources to see if there is any rumour about a Russian man being brought to the American embassy? That is all we need to know at the moment."

Malenkov said he understood and Bortsov went on to explain that if there were any clues to follow up, he would probably send one of his team to London to coordinate the inquiries. He added that meanwhile, he would be setting the same challenge to their people in the United States.

"The second task is something different," Bortsov continued. "You will know all about Yakov Rozovsky, of course, and he is about two years into his jail sentence there in the UK. Are you in touch with him?"

"Not personally," replied Igor Malenkov. "But he gets regular visits from the Defence attache here and our lawyers are still arguing the case with the British Foreign Office for his release. He is said to be in an open prison now, out in the countryside somewhere and staying well. I was here at the time, as you know, and it was more of a political case than a criminal one. I remember that Rozovsky was expected to get a top job back in Moscow when that stupid Russian Lieutenant business blew up. He should not have become involved, so why the interest now?"

"Yes, the bosses really want him back," replied Bortsov. "And they have asked us to identify a suitable VIP we can pick up on overseas travel on some pretext, preferably in Russia, and then detain them for a possible exchange deal for Rozovsky".

"Well, that's interesting and I already have a couple of ideas on this one," came the more enthusiastic reply from the London-based spook. "Give me a day or two to make some inquiries and check the details and I will get back to you."

"Sounds good," said Bortsov, who then added that he had assigned one if his brightest young agents called Egerov to move to the team in London where he had gained experience in his training. "One more head will be helpful to make it work," said Malenkov. And they continued to recall past experiences for a few minutes until he decided he needed to make his next call to Washington.

The Russian Federation Embassy in America's capital city is a group of large modern buildings behind high walls and gates on Wisconsin Avenue, a mile or so from Massachusetts Avenue which is known as "embassy row".   This was Russia's most important outpost and the Defence attache in charge of the GRU team was Dimitri Alexeyev, a name well known to Bortsov, but someone he had not previously encountered in his career.

However, the call went on much the same lines as the conversation with London. The issue of locating an abducted Russian was described in detail and Alexeyev listened intently and asked a few questions before telling Bortsov: "If it was the CIA who brought this man back to the States, my guess is that he would be taken to the agency's headquarters out in Virginia. It is a big operation there with many different sections including a group which specialises in Russian affairs. If he has some valuable knowledge or experience, this is where he would be interrogated".

He went on to describe the GRU operation in Washington and the network of informants they had created over the years. These included at least two with contacts inside the CIA and he thought that they would almost certainly hear any rumours about the arrival there of a Russian man. Bortsov explained that he wanted any inquiries to be very low key at this stage and that if they indicated a possible target, he would probably fly to Washington himself to coordinate the follow-up stages.

"The implications of this investigation are quite complex," he added. "And I will keep you informed at every stage of course. And we have a second challenge for you as well."

Bortsov then described the story of the diplomat in jail in the UK and the request from the top in the Kremlin to find a suitable hostage to be used in an exchange deal. Alexeyev nodded his understanding of this operation and replied: "Yes, we have done this before and this time I have an interest because I know Rozovsky very well and I was very concerned when I heard what had happened to him. We worked together in Moscow at one stage and then he had a spell at the embassy here before moving to London and it was a big surprise when he became involved in that problem with the British navy – so out of character that I think he was probably set up by MI5".

The conversation ended cordially with the diplomat in Washington agreeing to give both matters urgent attention and adding that he looked forward to welcoming Bortsov to the USA.

Chapter 18

An American Home

A few miles away at the Langley headquarters of the CIA, Lou Welensky had completed his training and met his new friend Alexa over breakfast in the staff restaurant on Saturday morning to plan their excursion into the neighbourhood in search of a suitable apartment. The Filipino lady explained that she had a former military colleague living in the nearby Falls Church area and that she would be moving into a shared house during the coming week. This friend might know of some possible options to consider but first they would check with the CIA administration office for further helpful information.

At this first stop, a helpful and typically efficient member of the staff had a file ready to share - with Lou's name on it! There was a street map of the local area, about a dozen leaflets from real estate companies describing available rental properties suitable for a single man, a listing of local amenities including food stores and movie theatres and even the names and contact details of two local lawyers who were familiar with helping new members of CIA staff. They were both impressed and appreciative of this level of assistance and after noting the addresses of several interesting apartment rentals, they soon set off on their familiarisation tour in Alexa's mini car.

As they left the entrance to the headquarters of the CIA, she turned left to join the treelined parkway towards the city of Washington. As they drove in the heavy morning traffic, Alexa described the sprawling area of Falls Church as a mainly residential suburb, conveniently located between the city and the state of Virginia. She explained that his made it an area favoured by many of the people working for international organizations in the capital, such as the World Bank, the International Monetary Fund and the many embassies in the city.

"This means that the local restaurants and food stores here cater very well for various international tastes," she continued, as they turned into a quiet road with a mixture or modern homes and then passed a large Safeway supermarket. "And there are various organizations and amenities like gyms and cafes which bring people together from many different nationalities."

Lou was feeling encouraged by this, which was far different from the Moscow city environment where he had previously lived during his time at GRU. They paused outside one of the apartment blocks in the brochures, where there was a vacancy on the third floor and in an attractive and quiet tree-lined road. They moved on to see the locations of two more possible homes, each looking impressive from an exterior viewing, and Alexa turned to Lou and asked him: "What do you think of Falls Church as your next home?"

He said he was impressed by everything in America and agreed to the suggestion that they should move on to the next residential area where Alexa explained that her friend had a 2-

bedroomed duplex property – in other words a house joined to the neighbouring home. They parked in the driveway of this attractive modern building with a flower garden and Alexa walked in after ringing the doorbell and called out: "We are here".

Lou tried to conceal his surprise when a tall, elegant black lady descended the stairs to the entrance lobby and welcomed Alexa with a warm hug. They then held hands as Alexa introduced her friend as Margo and went on to describe Lou as a new friend who she was helping to find an apartment. They were offered coffee in the smart, modern kitchen and spread the real estate brochures on the table to study together.

As the discussion continued, Lou could quickly see that Alexa and Margo were an "item" and found himself feeling quite relieved because during their time together, he had grown to enjoy Alexa's company and to recognise her attractive qualities. But again, he repeated to himself – "No more *femmes fatale*."

During the conversation, he discovered that the two ladies had served in the US Military police together, but that after five years of service they had the opportunity to retire and move on with their life together. Alexa said she had applied to join the CIA because she knew they were seeking more ethnic individuals in their ranks and also because she wanted more excitement and travel for a few years. Meanwhile, Margo had found an opportunity to join a DC-based security company as an investigator. So they were both in the learning stage with new careers as they prepared to set up a home together in Falls Church.

Their enthusiasm to describe their respective jobs and their plans for future social activities together in Washington meant that they took little interest in Lou's background story – other than to discover that his name revealed an East European parentage, which was hardly unusual in the USA. Neither were they very interested in the information he revealed in fragments of conversation that he had been brought up in New York by immigrant parents from Ukraine.

When they eventually decided to focus on his property brochures, Alexa took over the task of calling the real estate offices to make some viewing appointments. Two appointments to view apartments were confirmed for the afternoon so the threesome went out to a nearby Burger King for lunch and as the conversation began to include Lou, he told the ladies that he spoke some Russian and had worked in boring office jobs in the Big Apple. He discretely explained that he decided to look at jobs in the Washington area where his knowledge of Russian might be useful – and that was how he came to meet Alexa.

They squeezed into Alexa's car to find the two addresses which seemed of interest. Both apartments looked good to Lou, but it was Alexa who made the decision based on the condition of the kitchen and bathroom equipment, the colour scheme and the furnishings. The location also seemed to meet his needs – especially when Alexa offered to help him make the move. In fact, she added, she was actually planning to move into the nearby apartment she would now share with Margo during the next day.

The deal was done with the real estate agent, and the next stage was to shop for the essentials such as towels and bedding at a nearby mall with a homeware store. They did this together on the Sunday and on Monday morning, the administrative assistant at the CIA helped Lou with the rental paperwork and provided the information needed by the real estate agent.

And so Lou felt he had arrived, with a new American name and a new American home. He also collected an official envelope with confirmation of his new status with the CIA, together with instructions to report at 8.30 am the next day to David Boronavich, the head of the Russian section, to start his new job as an information analyst.

Chapter 19

A Surprise Murder Charge

As the chief of the GRU, Russia's secret intelligence agency – previously known as KGB - Yuri Bortsov's office in Moscow was busy with a flow of new challenges and old problems awaiting his attention. There was also a series of appointments and meetings with his superiors in the Kremlin and his senior colleagues. But he insisted to his assistant that anything related to his new 4-point plan of action got top priority.

Firstly, he focussed on Pavel Ilia's return from Japan, and submitting the official details for his new posting to the embassy in Washington DC, which needed authorisation from the US State Department. The young agent would become an assistant attache and it was probable that another member of the embassy staff would need to be reassigned to keep the head count at the embassy within the number agreed between the two governments. This was important because Bortsov believed that Ilia would play an essential part in the search for Aldanov.

Next, he read his briefing documents for the day and saw that his deputy, Dimitri Kotov, was top of his list of those seeking a meeting so he decided to escape from his desk and in-box and walked briskly to the next-door office – ordering his Expresso coffee on the way.

"So what's new?" he asked, settling into a comfortable chair.

"Some interesting developments about the woman spy you wanted us to follow up," Kotov began, getting his chief's immediate attention. "Apparently you asked our guys in Tokyo to make some more discreet inquiries. Well, it seems that they have established that a man and a woman went to the police centre where Aldanov was being interviewed on the evening before the court hearing about the shooting incident. According to their contact in the police, the couple were Americans and apparently they were allowed to meet Aldanov. So it is assumed that this is the same couple who then met him the next morning and took him off in the car."

"Yes, that all fits," replied Bortsov thoughtfully. "Our Ambassador in Tokyo told me that when it helps them, the Japanese and American intelligence people are thick as thieves. Have our people done any more work on that photograph taken by Ilia?"

"Some technical experts there have produced enlarged copies and apparently Ilia is being them with him when he flies back to Moscow tomorrow," came the answer. This was all positive news and they agreed that their own specialists in the GRU would be able to examine the photo and also work with the team which maintains personal records for all the known CIA operatives.

Bortsov told his deputy that this was a good start and they went on to discuss how to approach the two other challenges. Kotov said he had to make some quiet inquiries to check if there were any British or American suspects currently under investigation who might be candidates for a spy-swap, but had been met with a negative response. Neither was there any information about planned visits to Moscow in the near future from either country. They agreed that as discrete inquiries continued on all four targets, they would also start to make plans for Kotov to travel to London and Bortsov to Washington, together with Ilia, to work with the local GRU teams. The first objective for them both was to discover the current location of Aldanov and the second to discuss a possible exchange hostage.

The chief then added that he also wanted Kotov to also review the full story of Aldanov's disastrous visit to England two years earlier. "I still have a hunch that our mysterious female CIA agent was mixed up in that business in some way, so take a look through all the files from that event with our man Igor Malenkov. He is a good operator to have in London and he has a wide network of informers. And maybe you can see if either Igor or the Ambassador can arrange for you to visit Yakov Rozovsky in prison. There is still a lot we don't know, and he has had time to think about what happened."

As they began to discuss other matters which had occurred during the chief's brief absence in Tokyo, his assistant arrived and interrupted them to say there was an urgent call on the line from the embassy in Japan. Bortsov returned quickly to his desk and asked: "What's happening?"

It was Livitsky on the line and he explained that he was with the Russian Ambassador discussing an important new development. Then the Ambassador took over and began: "We are calling you first because you will understand the background. I have had a visit today from a minister in the Japanese justice department here to inform me that the other man involved in that shooting incident has died from his injuries after several weeks of intensive treatment. You may remember that his name was Hideki Endo and he was the locally-engaged administrative assistant to the naval attache. Well, the bottom line is that the two Japanese gunmen who were in court last week have now been charged with murder and there will be a new trial – and they want to recall our man Aldanov as a witness".

Bortsov and Kotov looked at each other and shook their heads in disbelief. "So what did you say, Mr. Ambassador?" asked the GRU chief.

General Malinov replied: "I expressed our condolences to Endo's family and explained that since Endo was an employee at the Russian embassy at the time of the incident, we would of course do anything possible to help and meet any costs involved. I also told him that there might be a problem regarding Aldanov's evidence, because we had recently reported to the Japanese police that he was a missing person."

The Ambassador went on to explain how this had come as a surprise to the minister who said he would have to consult the appropriate departments to discover the current status of the inquiry and would keep the Russian authorities informed of any developments. Bortsov said he was very sad to hear the news about Endo and then went on to update the General on his own search for the missing Aldanov who, he said. was now believed to be in the hands of the Americans, either in London or Washington.

"But don't tell the Japanese about that," Bortsov concluded. "Can I just suggest that if you need to tell them anything, you should say that we are also making extensive inquiries and will let them know if we find their missing witness."

General Malinov said he understood and would say the appropriate things in any future contacts with the minister from the justice department and also in his usual daily report to the foreign affairs office in Moscow.

Chapter 20

Vitamins and Ballet!

In the English countryside of Surrey, some 20 miles south-west of London, Sir Robert Briggs was in the study of his 18th century manor house reviewing his plans for a business visit to Russia in the following week. Winter was approaching and he began to wish he had arranged the trip a month earlier, before the threat of the first snowfall in Moscow. But appointments had been made with his agents there for a big contract to be signed for the export of a regular supply of his company's vitamin supplements into a new and growing market.

More than a decade earlier, Briggs had earned a first-class science degree at Cambridge University, followed by a year of business studies at Harvard in the USA. When he returned to the UK, he was head-hunted to join a newly established business which was preparing to enter the competitive health care sector. With the title of Business Development Director, it was a challenge he relished and he soon found a rented apartment in the town of Haslemere, not far from the company's new but small production and distribution centre.

The business had been set up by Angus McDermott, a former Scottish doctor who decided to retire early and pursue an opportunity to become an entrepreneur in the emerging market for vitamin supplements. He had lost his wife through cancer and this had led him to move south for a new challenge. He set up the business by renting a unit on an industrial estate near the small town of Haslemere and recruiting local staff. They installed the necessary equipment for production and packaging and as the business grew in the UK market he was able to buy and move into the spacious and elegant home he had previously discovered in the area.

His accountant advised him to recruit new management expertise and when Robert Briggs arrived, they began by analysing the existing production operations, the limited range currently being marketed and the recent sales performance figures. The new man soon found ways to introduce some of the experiences he had learned in the USA as he prepared a new business plan which involved new technologies and new on-line marketing methods. He also studied the competition and identified some possible new products and potential overseas markets. He carefully overcame his boss's Scottish reluctance to take financial risks and led a campaign among his contacts in the City to secure new investment. The results began to show and he was promoted to become Managing Director with Angus as chairman, and he was able to further strengthen the management team.

Along the way, Robert also became close to the chairman's only daughter, Annelise – and from her poise and presence he was not surprised to discover that she had trained as a ballerina until an injury forced her retirement at the age of 30. She was now working part-time in the small marketing department of her father's company, and she seemed to welcome the attentions of the new aggressive chief executive.

It was one evening over dinner in a local pub that they started to explore their possible future together and decided to tell her father that an engagement announcement was imminent. And it was during the same evening that Annelise told Robert that in her early dancing years, she was among a small group of English girls who had spent two-year training at the famous Bolshoi Ballet Academy in Moscow. "It was an amazing experience, so different from anything in London," she told him, adding: "And I made such good friends there and still stay in touch with some of them."

This triggered an idea in Robert's creative mind, who waited for the right moment in their romantic conversation to ask: "By the way, do you think your friends in Moscow could tell us about the possibilities for selling our products in the Russian market?"

In her recent activities in the company's marketing activity, Annelise had already been discussing international possibilities including expansion into the Nordic countries. But this was a new possibility which made her very thoughtful. "You might have something there," she told him, warming to the suggestion. "I think this is the sort of thing that the people involved in the ballet world might well find exciting. The Bolshoi has a huge following, of course, and perhaps we could create a new line of vitamins and then base a marketing project around the former ballerinas. Some of them are very well known."

From this dinner table discussion, a detailed plan emerged during the following days and because it was his daughter's idea, the usually ultra-cautious Scottish chairman agreed to them exploring it further. This was enough for Annelise to start the process by e-mailing one of her closest friends in Moscow suggesting a visit, and possibly also bringing her new fiancée to meet her. A warm and positive reply was enough for the dynamic Robert to then suggest that they could even plan to be married in the next weeks and then travel to Russia as part of their honeymoon.

It all worked – and it was Mr. and Mrs. Briggs who set off on their journey a month later starting with a week in romantic Vienna, followed by a week in Moscow. There, Annalise had arranged a lunch gathering with three of her friends who were also former dancers, and they soon became enthusiastic about their involvement in a project to introduce a new line of vitamin supplements. By a fortunate coincidence, one of them was working for a Russian advertising company and she was also able to introduce a bi-lingual commercial agent who met them the next day and he was happy to work out a deal to handle the marketing and distribution plans.

Back in Surrey, a new production line was set up, the packaging was redesigned in Russian and there was soon another trip to Moscow for the launch party which was organised by the agent, Vladimir. He had set up the event in a Moscow hotel with banners and brochures and when Robert Briggs was introduced, with an interpreter, he was supported by the photogenic group of well-known former ballerinas. Also there among the many carefully chosen guests invited by Vladimir was a Government minister from the Russian department of international trade who welcomed the arrival of a new business partnership.

Sadly, during the following day, the visit was interrupted by the news that Annelise's father had suffered a major heart attack and had died in hospital. The couple hastened their return home to deal with the many complex consequences of his sudden death – and ultimately, they were able to move together into the mansion which had been Angus McTavish's dream retirement home. They also found that in his will, he had left the controlling ownership of his company jointly to his only daughter and her husband.

It was a traumatic period for the wider family and all the local staff and friends, as well as many more distant relatives and friends who travelled from Scotland for the funeral. But as things went back to normal again, the business plan succeeded beyond their expectations and the names of their vitamin products became a by-word for success in many languages, including Russian.

The publicity surrounding this international expansion soon drew the name of Robert Briggs into recognition, first by membership of the London Chamber of Commerce and then at the Institute of Directors where this new, young entrepreneur was elected as a Board member. He became a favourite, inspirational after-dinner speaker and interviewee on radio and TV – and a year later his achievements were recognised in the Queen's Birthday Honours with a knighthood "for services to international business".

And so it was Sir Robert and Lady Briggs who set out for Moscow once again as the next winter approached to sign a new contract which would also open a marketing office in the city. This deal would effectively double the size of their company through the sales of new brands of vitamin supplements which were being introduced to Russia and other East European countries.

Chapter 21

Washington is the Target

\-

In Tokyo, Pavel Ilia was given 24-hoursnotice of his reassignment to Moscow and he was perplexed about the reason. He had served only three months of his two-year assignment and asked his bureau chief, Vitaly Livitsky, whether he had failed his last assignment by not staying closer to Aldanov or getting better photographic evidence of the abduction? He got a reassuring response and a reminder that even the GRU Director had been impressed by his account of the incident. Beyond that, he could not offer an explanation.

He was sad to be leaving as he said farewell to his colleagues and then collected his re-assignment documents and one-way air ticket from the administration office. After picking up all his personal belongings from his apartment he walked to the subway station for the train to Narita airport.

During the flight, he relaxed and recognised that he would now be seeing his family and friends again much sooner than he or they expected. His documents gave him two days to recover at his home after the long flight from Tokyo before reporting to Dimitri Kotov, the deputy chief of intelligence department at the Diamond. And he hoped he would be returning to the same group of colleagues where he had enjoyed his first two years with the department.

It was back into a familiar routine for Ilia when he took the underground train to the closest station to **Grizodubovoy Street to discover what was in store for him!** He had a warm welcome from his former colleagues who had heard about his unexpected return from Japan before going up to the next floor for his scheduled meeting with the deputy chief who greeted him cheerfully.

"Really good to see you again," said Kotov. "You probably wonder what this is all about, but we have some new top secret assignments and want you to be part of a small team working on one of them. After the last few weeks, you will probably not be surprised to know it is all about Nikolai Aldanov and it seems that you were the last person to see him in Japan so we need your input. Do you have the photographs?"

Ilia was relieved by this positive introduction and took the file from his briefcase containing a set of six images produced from his single shot of the group with Aldanov in Tokyo. Kotov took a quick look and grunted appreciatively with the instruction to take them later to a senior official in the technical services section who was expecting them. The boss then said forcefully: "This man Aldanov is a traitor and our task is to punish him in the only way."

Kotov had Ilia's full attention as he went on to describe what they knew so far about the events which had followed Aldanov's apparent abduction. He said that the evidence gathered in Tokyo indicated that it had been an American CIA operation to capture a man they knew to have been a former GRU agent and it was assumed that he had probably been flown out to either London or Washington. The assignment was to find him and to eliminate him before he could be of much value to the West. He went on to explain that the current stage was an investigation through their sources to discover whether a Russian had unexpectedly arrived to be questioned in one of those countries.

"When we discover which it is, we want you to join a small team to follow up and since he will probably be heavily disguised by the CIA, your recent knowledge will be essential in identifying our target," he explained, continuing: "You have talked to him and followed him and will know more about his personal characteristics than anyone else – and we also have his DNA profile from his time here in the department, so a final identification will also be your challenge."

Ilia felt increasingly confident and pleased to have been chosen for such a key operation and did not have any questions, other than about the likely timetable. Kotov told him: "We should get an answer in a day or two and then you should be ready to fly out to the UK or the USA to start the follow up actions. So keep your bags packed ready to go. We will have all the necessary paperwork and visa details sorted out for you – so you can relax at home until we call you and meanwhile, I will keep you up to date."

The next morning, Kotov reported on Ilia's return to Moscow at his regular briefing with the Director, Yuri Kortsov, and confirmed that he had briefed him on his new assignment.

"That's a good start," said the chief. "And what is more, it looks very much like a US operation. I have just had an update from Malenkov in London who says his team are pretty certain that no unexpected Russians have arrived at the US embassy in recent days. But a message from Alexeyev in Washington looks a bit

114

more promising. Apparently, a top CIA operations man has been in Japan and he flew back a couple of days ago in an air force plane so he could have secretly carried our man back to the US with him. Nothing further yet but I have a hunch that they have Aldanov in one of the CIA centres there by now and I have already asked our man to focus attention on his various contacts and informers there."

"So is it Ilia for Washington, then?" asked Kotov.

"Yes, and I am sure we can rely on Alexeyev," replied Bortsov." But this is important and I think you should bring forward your regular six monthly inspection visit to DC and take Ilia with you. So get all the paperwork sorted out and I will brief the Ambassador there when I know your timetable and also advise the Ministry people here. Okay?

Chapter 22

The Hostage

Challenge number three to find a 'hostage' was also on Bortsov's mind. He had decided not to complicate his phone calls to London and Washington with this issue as well, so when he had a quiet moment later the same day, he decided to call a personal friend Alexi in the international business ministry for an informal chat. After exchanging news about their jobs and families, he asked if there might be any important events in the near future which might bring British delegates to Moscow.

"No big exhibitions or conferences that I know about," came the reply, but after a moment's thought, Alexi added that there would be an event in the following week to launch a new British health product into the Russian market. He added that his minister had been invited. "It does not look like a big deal," he added. "Something to do with vitamins, can you believe that? But the minister has accepted the invitation because the boss of the company is well-connected in the London business and political circles and is regarded as a useful contact. So what's your interest, Yuri?"

"Not vitamins, I can assure you," came the reply, with a laugh. "It's just that we need to build one or two new contacts in the

UK and these business events often prove productive. This happens to be quite timely for us, so where is this thing taking place?"

"It's at the Ritz-Carlton hotel on Wednesday morning and I know they have a local marketing agency arranging everything – but that's all I know."

Yuri Bortsov ended the conversation thinking this might be his lucky day. He asked his assistant to call the Ritz Carlton and find the name of the company organising the vitamins promotion event in the next week and she soon returned with the details of the agency and the name of the executive handling the arrangements. "Get him on the line?" he asked.

The PR man was not surprised to get a call from the secret services ahead of an international event and he was flattered to find himself talking to the GRU Director. He was happy to pass on the information that the visiting VIP from London was Sir Robert Briggs and that he would be in Moscow for three or four days with his wife, Lady Briggs who, he added, had trained at the Bolshoi Academy as a ballerina some ten years previously – which would help to make it a good news story. The couple would be staying at a suite in the same hotel as the event he was organising for the company on Wednesday morning. This was all that Bortsov needed to know, and he decided that his target would be Lady Briggs because her detention by GRU would be bigger headlines in Britain as well as in Mocow and that her husband would be most effective in putting pressure on the authorities in London to secure her release. But first he needed to get his research team working on the background of the Briggs family and their business activities. He also assigned one of his agents to track the couple closely when they arrived in Moscow, to report on exactly who they met during their stay, and also to bug their hotel suite.

It all went as planned and Bortsov had a file of information to review on the day before the British vitamins marketing event. It all seemed like a perfect match for his objective, and he had a meeting with his experienced agent to discuss tactics. The agent reported that the couple had arrived at the hotel the previous day and while the man was busy with his local marketing representatives, his wife had been meeting with several women who he understood were also former Bolshoi dancers. She had also met a man who he knew to be the Moscow-based correspondent of the BBC and two other men he had not identified – but who he assumed were also from the media.

Bortsov decided that this was enough, and he gave the agent his instructions: "When they check out from the hotel, arrange to have two uniformed police with you and when the couple are outside the building you should identify yourself and tell Lady Briggs that she is under arrest for breaches of security regulations. You will tell the police officers to take her to the nearest police station and charge her accordingly and then await further instructions. No doubt her husband will create a great protest and ask to speak to the British Ambassador. You can advise him to use his waiting airport limousine and to continue his journey home but he will probably refuse to go without his wife – so just let him go back into the hotel and he can contact his Embassy from there."

The agent seemed to understand the plan and said he would report back on any changes in the arrangements. He would also be ready to follow the police car and at the police station he would ensure that the charge was properly explained to the woman and added that he would ask the custody officer to ensure that she was carefully looked after.

"That sounds spot on," replied Bortsov. "Then we will stand by for the reactions from the British embassy and from London. And we will also make a statement for the media people to be released tomorrow, after they have done their reports on the vitamins thing at the Ritz Carlton. With all those ballerinas involved as well, it will create some headlines and pictures here and around the world, which is just what we want."

In a hotel conference room the next morning, Sir Robert and his wife were joined at the appointed hour by the Russian international trade minister and two of his staff. There was a plinth decorated with bold, colourful banners announcing the new vitamin supplements. There were handouts and sample packages for the dozen or so reporters and cameramen who were gathered for the event, as well as more than 25 local businessmen invited by the local marketing agent to hear the upbeat health messages delivered by the company chairman and the minister. They all posed cheerfully with six elegant former ballerinas and Sir Robert was upbeat and positive in his interviews with the press, radio and TV reporters.

The British couple relaxed with two of Lady Briggs' friends for a light lunch until a message arrived that their car was waiting to take them to the airport. In the hotel lobby, Lady Briggs stopped for a final few words with her Russian friends as her husband went out to check that the car was ready – but to his surprise, she did not immediately follow him. He looked at his watch

119

anxiously, then went back inside to see the two dancer friends looking perplexed. "Where is Annelise?" he asked. They explained in their halting English that she had been arrested by two policemen and taken out of the hotel by a back door. One of them added: "It all happened so quickly. She called back to us to find you but that's all we know."

They were clearly frightened, but Sir Robert tried to reassure them that it was not their fault and he dashed off to find the hotel manager's office. The manager knew nothing, but when he heard the story, he sent for his security manager to give any assistance – and then the forlorn Englishman dialled the number of the Ambassador's office at British Embassy to report to the secretary what had happened.

Sir Humphrey Michaels, the British Ambassador himself no less, arrived at the hotel in less than 15 minutes and after a brief chat with the confused businessman in the foyer he realised that this was a major diplomatic issue. He made a quick call to his office and without any delay, they set off together in the embassy limousine, with its small Union Jack, fluttering to the Russian Foreign Office for a hastily arranged appointment with a deputy minister. On the way, the diplomat tried to reassure his visitor that this was far from being the first time that something like this had occurred. He explained that he would lodge an official protest against an unlawful arrest, obtain access for a lawyer to meet with Lady Briggs immediately, seek a release on bail while the matter was being processed, and ask for her to be reunited with her husband. He would also ask for more background information about the arrest and then as they approached the huge government building in Red Square, he advised Sir Robert: "I appreciate that you are angry and offended by this unexpected turn of events, but please try to let me do the talking at our meeting."

As expected, the meeting was polite and brief, and the Ambassador explained why Sir Robert Briggs and his wife were in Moscow and added that they had made previous business visits during recent years and had good friends in the city. Briggs was surprised to hear through an interpreter that the Russian minister appeared to know nothing about the event at the Ritz Carlton hotel. He watched carefully as the Russian's assistant made careful notes of everything that was said, and the minister promised an initial response before the end of the day. Finally, he asked for an assurance that Sir Robert was not now planning to fly back to the UK that evening and would remain at the hotel.

In the car on the way back to the Ritz Carlton, the Ambassador said: "You probably realised that the minister knew more about this than he was admitting. He even knew that you were planning to fly back to the UK today. But this is not unusual. They tend to keep their cards close to their chest."

"Yes, I am getting the picture," replied Briggs and as they arrived back at the hotel, he said he was sure they would find him a room and also remembered that he needed to let BA know that they would not be on their London flight that evening and would need a new reservation. Before driving away, the Ambassador said they would call him with any new information – "But meanwhile, leave it to us and have a good sleep – we will have another chat in the morning."

Chapter 23

The Search Begins

Kotov and Ilia flew business class on the nine-hour flight from Moscow to Washington and at Dulles airport they were welcomed warmly in the arrivals hall by Dimitri Alexeyev from the Russian embassy. They had diplomatic visas so there was no delay with immigration formalities, and they were soon on their way by car into the city and the Georgetown Hotel on Wisconsin Avenue, not far from the Embassy.

"We will talk about business tomorrow when you have had a rest and recovered from the time change," said Alexeyev as he described some of the features they passed during the half hour drive. He had noted that it was Ilia's first visit to the USA and added: "It's a nice country really – pity about the Americans. They have some strange ways and don't really like foreigners."

Ilia was impressed by the number of new technology companies with impressive tower blocks alongside the airport freeway. And then the red brick buildings of the Georgetown University as they crossed the Potomac river bridge and drove through the busy and more traditional Georgetown area to the door of the hotel. "It is not what I expected," he ventured. "I have only seen

America in movies and news coverage, and it all looks more interesting than I thought."

As they took their luggage from the car, Kotov told him: "Don't worry. I think we will be here for some time on this assignment so you will be able to see much more of Washington".

The next morning, they walked half a mile up Wisconsin Avenue to the high walls surrounding the Russian embassy and showed their identity documents to the guard at the iron gated entrance. He made a phone call and after a couple of minutes, Dimitri Alexeyev was there to collect them. He was a defence department attache as well as the GRU bureau chief and he greeted Dimitri Kotov as a long-time colleague and friend before he was introduced to Pavel Ilia. As they walked together across the courtyard towards the main building, Ilia could not help but be impressed by the array of antennas and satellite dishes on the rooftops – more than he had seen anywhere previously, he thought.

After a catching-up chat with coffee in the cafeteria, their first stop was a 10am appointment with the Ambassador which was brief and quite formal as he emphasised to them that the only people who knew about their special assignment, apart from Alexeyev and himself, were Kotov and Ilia. "So keep me informed," he emphasised as they departed.

In the bureau chief's office, they began to consider a plan of action. Kotov was the senior member of the group and he took the lead: "We are only assuming that our man Aldanov is in Washington but in the absence of any other evidence, we believe the CIA picked him up in Japan and spirited him away so this is the most likely place for them to hide him. So Dimitri, what does your local background experience tell you?"

Alexeyev took this as a cue to show his detailed knowledge about the CIA structure and its headquarters at Langley, a few miles out of the city in Virginia. He explained how he and his predecessors had built up a small but crucial network of informants who in turn had other contacts among those providing various services to the CIA – "everything from cleaners to drivers and even interpreters", he explained. He also emphasised the size of the organization and the hundreds of personnel based there, including a special section focussing on Russian activities. "That is where they will be holding Aldanov, if he is here at all," he added and continued: "The interrogators will be de-briefing him on everything he knows about our operations in Moscow."

The group decided that the next stage in their quest should therefore be a briefing for the locally-based team of four GRU agents reporting to Alexeyev. He agreed to instruct them to focus their efforts on discretely contacting their most likely informers to ask if they had heard of a new Russian man arriving in the city in recent weeks. "It will take a week or two, but between them, they seem to know about all the comings and goings of foreigners," he added, optimistically, then adding: "So what happens next?"

"We suspect that the intelligence agency people will get their hands on him and after a de-briefing, the Americans may even use Aldanov's previous experience in their operations in some way – and maybe hide him with a new identity and appearance. And this is where you come in Ilia," responded Kotov. "If we do identify a possible target individual, your job will be to follow up any new information about his movements and then to tail him as closely as possible"

Then turning back to Alexeyev, he added: "Ilia is the last person we have who spent time with Aldanov before he disappeared in Tokyo so he will also need to be disguised so far as possible to avoid recognition – and as you can see, he already has a week's growth of facial hair as a start."

Ilia stroked his chin and moustache with a smile and then added: "I will get a couple of hats as well. So what do I do next?"

"When you have a target to follow, Ilia," continued Kotov, "Your aim is to get a DNA confirmation in one of the many ways you studied in your training – coffee cups, door handles and so on – and then if we get a positive match, we will know that we have our man. Then the next move will be a decision which will be made by the Ambassador here, in liaison with Yuri Kortsov in Moscow, of course."

They agreed that the three of them would meet up at 9am each morning for an update, but would stay in phone contact for any urgent developments – otherwise, Ilia would relax at the Georgetown hotel with Kotov and he was free to enjoy his first visit to Washington DC.

For more than a week, the daily meetings had no new developments to review and Ilia had the time to explore the Smithsonian museums, the art galleries and the various tourist attractions of the American capital. He paid two visits to the Air and Space Museum and took a half day excursion together with Kotov to see George Washington's historic home on the banks of the Potomac River at Mount Vernon. He was becoming impressed by everything and told his colleague that he would like his next assignment to be two years in the USA instead of returning to Japan.

"Let's get this job done first," was he firm reply.

Chapter 24

Charged with Spying

After a restless night on his own at the hotel, Sir Robert was woken at 7 am by a phone call from an attache at the British Embassy. He introduced himself as Robin Charters and said he had been assigned by the Ambassador to follow up on the incident and provide any help which may be needed. He went on to inform Sir Robert that he had identified the police station where Lady Briggs was being held and that he would be going there at 8.30 am with a Russian lawyer who worked for the embassy on such matters.

"Can I come with you to see my wife?" asked a desperate Sir Robert, but he was told that it would be unwise at this stage and that he should remain at the hotel for a further follow up call later – "As soon as I have some news for you," said the calm English voice.

Sir Robert ordered coffee and a light breakfast and dressed to prepare for an uncertain day. The only person he could call while he was waiting was his Moscow marketing agent who he discovered knew nothing about the detention of Annelise the previous day. He was alarmed by the development, but as a Russian, he clearly did not want to become involved and went on to report that there had been good coverage in the press and on radio from the product launch – but this was far from Robert's mind at this time. He watched some Russian news channels … and waited.

Around 10 am, Robin Charters was on the phone. "I am downstairs in the lobby with our lawyer. Can you join us in the coffee shop for an update?"

Sir Robert was immediately recognised as he walked in and the young diplomat took him to a quiet corner booth where he introduced Sergei Oblomov as "our local bi-lingual lawyer who is experienced in these diplomatic matters."

"It's like this," began Robin Charters. "When we arrived at the police station, Sergei was told that your wife is facing charges of seeking secret information from people she met during her visit. We were allowed to talk to her for about ten minutes and she is well but somewhat confused because the officers she saw last night did not speak any English. We tried to reassure her and said we are doing everything we can to help her and advised her to say as little as possible, other than confirming her name and requesting an interpreter at any further interviews. They have taken her passport but her holding cell is relatively comfortable and she said she had managed to get some sleep. Apparently, they took coffee and cookies to her this morning. She sends you her love and says not to worry".

Sir Robert nodded appreciatively, and Robin went on to say that Sergei then had a meeting with a senior police officer who told him that this was a very serious matter and that there were a number of inquiries to be made with all the lady's contacts in Moscow before formal charges are brought.

"In my experience, this is going to take a couple of weeks at least," explained Sergei. "And I can certainly try to get the lady released on some sort of house arrest during this period. But she would have a police guard 24-hours a day and only be allowed very limited contacts. Is there anywhere she can go which meets these requirements?"

"Not that I know of, so when can I go to see my wife" interrupted Sir Richard, who was trying hard to conceal his anger and to stay calm and composed. Then after a pause, he added: "You may not know this, but we are actually on our honeymoon. We were married in London ten days ago and had a week together in Vienna before coming to Moscow."

"Well, I suppose congratulations are in order," said Robin. "I realise that this is really terrible for you, sir. As it happens, we do have a couple of small apartments near the embassy we use for visitors and I think we could make one of these available for your wife it if meets the requirements of the authorities. What do you think, Sergei?"

The Russian lawyer said he would go back to the police station at once and seek a meeting with the area police commissioner to submit two formal requests – firstly to allow her husband to visit her and secondly to propose her move to the embassy apartment for the period of house arrest, which he hoped would be as brief as possible. Then he added reassuringly to Richard: "I will also insist to them that this is all a dreadful mistake and that your wife has not committed any security breaches."

Robin Charters suggested that while this was taking place, he and Sir Richard should go to the British embassy to review the situation with the Ambassador and also their own experts on such matters, while they waited for an update from Sergei Oblomov. Sir Richard was greeted sympathetically by the Ambassador, and they were joined by two senior diplomats who were introduced as defence attaches. One of them added quietly that he also worked for the intelligence service, "better known as MI6". While the group was being briefed on the background, they were interrupted by a call from Sergei Oblomov who told them that the police chief had shown an unexpected "soft spot" when he was told about the honeymoon trip and had agreed that a short visit to Lady Briggs by her husband would be possible in one hour's time. He also added that they would consider the proposal for house arrest at a British embassy apartment but not to expect a reply for a day or two while further questioning of witnesses took place.

"So what do I do next?" asked Sir Richard and he was surprised to be advised by the MI6 man to return to London on his own as quickly as possible – "Before they decide to implicate you in these intelligence matters as well – and they are probably fake anyway".

The Ambassador said he agreed and went on: "I am sorry to say this to you Richard, but this could take a few weeks to sort out and we will do everything we can to take good care of your wife. Also bear in mind that this will soon leak to the media. I understand that you have good contacts in London so your best contribution will be to use them in clearing your wife's name and looking after your business. You will also be important in working with the Foreign Office to secure her release as soon as possible. Much as it goes against your instincts and personal feelings, I believe you will be able to do much more in London than you can here".

Sir Richard looked confused by this sudden turn of events but after collecting his thoughts, he reluctantly agreed that it made sense and the Ambassador continued: "I suggest you go with Robin to see your wife now. But here is something very important - the Ruskis will listen in to your conversation so do not, repeat not, mention that you are returning to London. Just go off now in our car, pick up your bags at the hotel and go straight to the airport after seeing Lady Briggs. We will let our lawyer know you are on the way and my assistant will book you a seat on the early afternoon BA flight to London, so bon voyage. Does that all sound okay?"

The MI6 man interrupted again and offered some further advice: "I suggest that when you stop at the Ritz Carlton you just collect a few things your wife might need and maybe your briefcase. But leave everything else in your room as if you are staying. Later on we will arrange to check you out of the hotel and pick up all your baggage, but not until we are sure that you are on the plane to London".

The Ambassador agreed that this was a sensible precaution. There were farewell handshakes all round and Robin led the way to an embassy car waiting at a rear exit ready to take the two of them to the police station. On the way, Sir Richard tried to appear casual when they stopped at the hotel and he went up to his room. He quickly put together a bag of Annelise's bag toiletries and a few items of clean clothes, picked up his documents case, and then strolled calmly out to the car to continue his journey.

Sergei was there to meet them in the police station waiting room and after a quick briefing from the lawyer, a uniformed escort arrived who checked Sir Richard's bags and pockets thoroughly before leading him alone to the cell block where he was told he could spend 15 minutes with his wife before her next interview. He took a deep breath and made an effort to compose himself as a guard unlocked a cell door and there, slumped on the edge of the small single bed was his Annelise ....

She could hardly believe her eyes and as she pulled herself up she began to cry as she embraced Richard and asked: "Can we go now, darling?"

It was a minute or so as they kissed and hugged without any more words. And before he replied, he used his best sign language to indicate to her that the Russians were listening and could probably hear every word they said. "Not just yet," said Richard, as he comforted her. "This is rather a serious business and I know none of it is true. But they say that you have been asking sensitive political questions in your meetings with your friends and they say have to check it out before deciding whether to charge you with doing anything wrong and this may take a few days."

"A few days – in here?" she answered anxiously. And then, trying hard to pull herself together she told him: "The police should not have any problems. I had much more interesting things to talk to my friends about and I am sure they will all confirm this."

"Yes, I am sure as well, but don't worry," he replied, reassuringly. "I have been with the British Ambassador today and he has some very good people here with experience of these things and they will be in touch with you and look after your interests. The Russian police were very kind and allowed me to come and visit you today but I am not sure what happens next. The embassy's lawyer is also here with me, and he is trying to work out whether they will let you move into one of the embassy guest flats while the inquiries are being made"

Annelise asked him why they could not just stay together in the hotel for a few more days while things are being sorted out and her husband explained that it was not possible because she would be under what they called "house arrest". But since she did not have a house in Moscow, they were considering this alternative.

"It would be much more comfortable, of course," explained Richard. "But there will have to be a poiice guard and you will not be allowed out or see any visitors other than those involved in the legal case until they have decided whether or not they have a case. But I promise we will all be working on helping you – the people at the embassy here and at the Foreign Office back in London and we will stay in touch as much as possible."

Richard then showed his wife the bag of toiletries and clothes he had brought with him for his wife, and she began to realise the seriousness of her situation. "I will try to be strong," she reassured him as the guard opened the door to indicate that their 15 minutes had elapsed.

With time only for another hug and kiss, he was escorted out of the cell and turned in alarm as the door closed noisily behind him. Robin and the lawyer reassured him that he was doing the best thing possible as they went briskly to the car park, watched closely by the Police. There, the car was waiting to take Sir Richard and Robin to the airport where his ticket was waiting at the British Airways check-in desk and the boarding procedures went smoothly. After a brief farewell, Robin waited anxiously in a quiet corner of the terminal until he saw the aircraft taxi out to the runway and take off – much to his relief.

Chapter 25

Is It Aldanov?

The morning eventually came at the Russian Embassy in Washington DC when the chief of the GRU section, Dimitri Alexeyev, eagerly greeted his two colleagues from Moscow at their regular meeting in his office and announced: "I think we have a hit".

Kotov and Ilia had tried to be patient as each day passed, but with this news they soon became alert and focussed as he went on to describe how one of his most experienced female agents called Alina had been quietly spreading the word around her most discrete contacts about their interest in finding a newly-arrived Russian man in the city. She had got their attention when she told them "in great confidence" that this mystery man might be in contact with the CIA. The positive information had eventually come from someone working in the city's largest security services company – "which of course is a good place for us to have informants anyway", he explained.

"This contact led to our agent finding an opportunity for a quiet word with one of their PR staff called Margo, who had a very interesting tale to tell," continued Alexeyev. "She told Alina that one of her close friends actually worked at the CIA in Langley and that she was currently helping one of her new friends to find some place to live. He apparently had a Russian background and she had guessed that he might be a new recruit to the agency. So this sounded like a positive lead to follow up".

He then continued with more details and told them: "I asked my agent to check carefully that this Margo woman was not a security risk and if it all looked safe, then she should arrange a confidential rendezvous where we could meet her together. It turned out that Margo's friend at the CIA is actually her long-time partner and that they live together in an apartment in Falls Church. So if we pursue this any further, we will have to ensure that they both understand that they are bound by the official secrets rules".

Alexeyev said he had been reassured by some further research which showed that the two women had actually met when they both served in the US Military Police. They had retired from the service with clean records after five years to embark on new careers and to make their new life together. So he had already decided to go ahead and have a meeting with Margo and Ilina, which took place in the quiet lounge of Georgetown's Four Seasons Hotel just the previous day.

"This Margo is an impressive lady," he said. "She understood the basis on which she was talking to us and did not seem to have any particular prejudice against Russians – like some Americans do. Anyway, she was able to tell us that she had actually met the Russian man in question when she and her partner took him to view some vacant rental apartments in the same area where they lived, Falls Church. He had been introduced to her as Lou and she had found him to be a very personable and intelligent man in his late 30's. "But he was rather over-keen on impressing me," she added. "And I did not trust everything he said."

She also told them that she did not discover much about his background, except that he seemed to be new to the USA and had a Russian ancestry. She also said because of the Russian links, she could appreciate why the American intelligence people might find him useful. She went on to describe how the two ladies had apparently advised him about which apartment he should choose and added that he then went ahead with the real estate representative and signed up. She also heard that he had already fixed a date to move in. She also provided a partial description of him as a medium height man, slim build and with a smallish beard… and she even gave us his new address."

Dimitri Kotov was impressed, but cautious. "This is very interesting work, but it is not conclusive," he commented. "Did she actually realise that she was helping us?" he asked. And Alexeyev told him that strangely, perhaps, she had seemed to be more concerned that this man was being disloyal, which went against her principles.

"Right," said Kotov. "I think it is now over to Ilia to try to check this man out and see if we can identify him as our target."

He went on to explain to his two colleagues that the next stage would be for Ilia to use his skills to set up a trail on the man in their sights and look for signs of identification. It was agreed that he would rent a small car for a month and that Alina would go with him to visit the area, which she knew well. Ilia agreed that this would be a good start and they agreed that he would find the best way to keep a discrete watch on the man's arrivals and departures from the apartment he had rented. The aim was that ultimately, he would need to find an opportunity to obtain a DNA sample by one means or another.

The group went on to discuss ways in which this might be achieved, and it was agreed that Ilia should vary his presence in the area by having Alina accompany him from time to time. Hopefully, they could follow their target when he walked to the nearby shopping mall where there was a food store, several takeaway food shops and at least two cafes.

"I get the idea," said Ilia, confidently. "It seems that we will be looking for used cups, cigarette butts if he smokes like most Russians, or we may have to search his trash or maybe take swabs from anything he handles."

"Yes, that's it," said Alexeyev. "And we have a lab here which can test any DNA samples and they will set you up with small containers and plastic bags to use. But first things first. Let's find out when he actually moves into the Falls Church apartment. That's a job Alina can do for starters."

He called her office number and within a few minutes, they were joined by the GRU agent – a small, trim and athletic-looking lady in her 40s. She was introduced to the group and gave Ilia a specially warm welcome as a fellow spook and said she looked forward to working with him. She already knew part of the story after being involved in the meeting with Margo from the security company and she listened intently as her chief outlined the plan of action.

"I get the picture," she replied confidently. "I will get together with Ilia on the details and we will get to work as soon as I find out when our mystery man is moving into the apartment".

Then turning to Alia and taking his arm, she added: "Let's go down to my office and make a start."

Chapter 26

Front page news

Sir Robert Briggs had a restless flight back to Heathrow as he tried to come to terms with the unexpected events of the past 24 hours and the image in his mind of Annelise in the police cell. A Scotch helped but he did not eat much of the meal served to him by an attentive flight attendant in the first class cabin. He had no baggage to collect and he was uncertain about what to do next or where to go as he followed the signs to the exit. It came as a great relief when he was met in the airport arrivals area by a smartly dressed youngish man who recognised him and introduced himself as "Turner, Denis Turner, from the Foreign Office."

They walked briskly to the car park where he was asked: "To your home in Surrey, I presume, sir?" Sir Robert agreed and as they drove out towards the motorway, Turner explained that he was actually with the MI6 East European section and was one of the small team working on the problem of the detention of Lady Briggs in Moscow. He clearly knew all the facts and said he had been briefed that afternoon by the British Ambassador on the next steps. He was able to discuss the details until they came to the manor house near Haslemere, when he concluded: "I suggest you get a night's sleep, sir, and then come up to London by train in the morning. Let me know your arrival time and I will meet you at Waterloo – and by the way, it seems that the media have got hold of the news about your wife and it may be in tomorrow's newspapers."

It was already 10pm when Sir Robert let himself into the empty house and decided he had to talk to someone. So he went to his study and called Henry Withers, his company's managing director and began to apologise for disturbing him but was quickly interrupted.

"Where are you Robert and what the heck is going on??" he asked.

"I am back at home, Hank – just arrived and I am on my own," came the reply.

"Well, my day began with great news about the product launch in Moscow yesterday", said Henry Withers. "But this evening I have been getting calls from the press telling me that Annelise has been arrested by the Russians as a suspected spy. That came as a huge shock, of course, and all I could say was that I knew you had both been in Russia but that I had no other information. So is this true?"

"I'm afraid it is," replied Robert. "And I was advised by the British embassy people to fly back on my own before I became implicated as well and to leave it to them to sort out the crazy legal business. And it was hard to leave Annelise in a cell at the police station with armed guards outside."

"My god, I am so sorry Robert. How did this all happen?"

Robert went on to describe all the events of the day in detail and told his colleague how he had been met at Heathrow by a man from MI6 who drove him home. On the way, he had heard more details which had underlined the seriousness of the situation and he added that he would be going on an early train to London in the morning. He would then be met at Waterloo to go to the Security Services headquarters in London to discuss what happens next. "And now," he added, "I will leave my phone off the hook, open a can of beans and try to get some sleep … and I will call you some time tomorrow."

It was 7.30 in the morning when Robert parked his car at the station, bought a coffee and bacon sandwich at the café together with a copy of The Daily Telegraph, and found a seat in the first-class coach with the commuters on a crowded train to Waterloo. As he enjoyed his breakfast, he looked at his paper and was alarmed to see a headline at the foot of the front page:

"British businessman's wife detained in Moscow on spying charges – on their honeymoon! – See details on p3."

He then phoned the number which his MI5 contact had given him and gave Turner his train arrival details. Then he opened up page 3 without attracting the attention of his fellow passengers and soon found a carefully worded report with the same headline. It described accurately how he and his wife had travelled to Moscow for a business event after honeymooning in Vienna. It went on to say that as the couple were leaving their hotel to fly back to London, Lady Annelise Briggs had been arrested by two armed Russian police officers and taken to a nearby police station. The British embassy had confirmed only that she was being questioned for allegedly seeking secret information and that they were urgently demanding her release. He was gratified to find that the report then finished with details of the Briggs company's new vitamin supplements deal for the Russian market, together with a photograph of the couple at the event with the group of elegant former ballerinas.

Sir Robert gave sigh of relief that there was nothing too damaging or contentious in this report – but he wondered what the tabloid press were making of it? And what would come next?

At Waterloo, his MI6 contact Turner was waiting on the platform and took him swiftly to a waiting car and they sped away to the Thameside building which houses the UK's intelligence services. On the way he said he had seen the newspaper report and agreed that they would need to discuss how to handle any future statements to the media. "That is on our agenda this morning," said Turner.

After security checks at the entrance, the two men went up to a second-floor conference room where they were joined by Florence McIver, who introduced herself as a Deputy Director and Denis Turner said he was a Russia specialist in the department. They began by quizzing Robert in great detail about his wife's background, her interests and her Russian contacts.

He answered all the questions and emphasised that her Russian links were only in the area of her special ballet interests and her time at the Bolshoi academy in Moscow. He concluded by telling them: "I have known Annelise and her father since I joined the company about five years ago and neither of them have shown any interest in political activities – and certainly not Russian or communist matters. Mr. McDermott is a hard-working Scottish entrepreneur and his daughter takes after him in many ways.

Since giving up her dancing career, she has been involved in growing his business and our relationship developed in the past year as I described. If she had carried any left-wing tendencies, they would have been totally alien to me and I would certainly have known by now".

The group then turned to the next moves and the Deputy Director said she was advising the Foreign Office on their response to the Russian authorities. "Basically, they are insisting on her total innocence and emphasising that they must have made a mistake and should release her without delay". She then shared the new information that the Russians had compromised a by allowing her to move to a British embassy apartment but remaining under house arrest while they complete their investigations, which Robert welcomed as a bit of good news. The Foreign Office had also told her that the Ambassador in Moscow suspected that the Russians had some other motive for making this arrest – "We are urgently looking at all the precedents and possible options", she added.

Finally, the three of them discussed the question of media coverage. Dennis Turner said the Foreign Office press department was preparing a statement, adding that they were also considering if and when it might be helpful for Sir Robert to do a radio and TV interview to give the coverage a 'human face'. He then decided to call his contact there to see if they needed any further information.

The press officer came on the speaker phone and said she had been trying to call Sir Robert to clarify some of the details about his wife. He provided the answers and then asked whether he should answer any calls he might get from the media? "I think you should be helpful to them, unless they become a nuisance," she told him. "I am sure that anything you say will emphasise that this must all be a terrible mistake and that Annelise is the last person to be involved in spying".

She warned the group that this was certain to be a big story for the next few days and support from the press and the public would help her bosses at the Foreign Office and at the Moscow embassy in their negotiations with the Russians. They were urgently seeking for the matter to be dropped and for the lady to be released as quickly as possible.

Sir Robert said he would do "whatever it takes to help" and Florence McIver encourage him to return to his home or his business and try to relax and wait for further news.

Chapter 27

Eliminate the Traitor!

Yuri Bortsov went to his regular weekly meeting with his boss General Yazof, the Deputy Minister, in his elegant office in the top floor of the Defence Department, adjoining the Kremlin. After hearing the usual briefing on government policy matters, Birtsov decided it was time to provide a progress report on what he described as "his four-point retaliation plan".

"Firstly, our team has been in Washington DC for over two weeks and we are now pretty sure that Aldanov is there and possibly in the hands of the CIA, as we expected," he began. "They have done some smart work through the local network and believe they have identified a suspect there with a new name and a new identity. This man certainly has a Russian background and the crucial stage now is getting a DNA match and they are working on it. The question then will be what action do we take?"

"You know the answer to that," replied the General brusquely. "He is a traitor and there is only one action and that will be authorised at the appropriate time by the Kremlin. So prepare an appropriate plan to eliminate him when you are sure you have the right man."

Bortsov nodded to confirm that he understood his instructions and then went on to describe the progress on the second part of his plan.

"As you may have heard, we have our hostage," he said. "It is certain to get the British authorities worked up because it is the wife of an aristocratic businessman, name of Lady Annelise Briggs. She and her husband were here for a relatively minor business event, something to do with selling their vitamin supplements, I believe. It was discovered that she knows quite a few Russians after spending some time here at the Bolshoi Academy in her younger days and the security people are busy building a strong case against her for seeking secret information in all the meetings she had with her contacts while they were here for two or three days at the Ritz Carlton hotel. What is more is the discovery that the couple were married a couple of weeks ago and this trip was part of their honeymoon."

General Yazov laughed this time. "Vitamins and ballet dancing? And interrupting a honeymoon? What are you getting mixed up with now?" he asked.

"Don't worry," replied Bortsov. "It all sounds very innocent. But the couple are well-connected back in London and there will be a big fuss in the press about the arrest of this lady and the accusation of spying. You can be sure that the Foreign Office in London will be under a lot of pressure to get her back home. So I suggest that you just wait a few days, and then talk to your colleagues in the foreign affairs directorate about negotiating to get Yazov Rozovsky out of the English prison at last. He has served over two years, so they have had their pound of flesh."

"Good – I like your thinking," said the General. "So far so good. What next?"

Bortsov then went on to describe in detail how the next stages in his plans would also switch to the UK where he had two more objectives. He recalled how in his original briefing to the General, he had said that his number one plan was to identify a target for a major hit on the country's security systems which would demonstrate the strength of the GRU. He said he had researched some possibilities and would be reviewing them in detail with their bureau chief in London. When he had drawn up an action plan, he said he would review it with the General to get approval.

After that, he would be focussing on his aim of tracking down the MI5 and CIA operators who had worked together to defeat the original and seriously flawed Aldanov plan for recruiting an informant in the British navy - and he would then carry out an appropriate reprisal.

"For this activity, I am hoping to get some valuable input from Rozovsky when we get him back," continued Bortsov. "He was our top man in London at the time and there must be some information in his files or in his memory which will help us. He must have had some very good reason for going to that funeral for the British girl who met Aldanov – that was the Ricin poisoning project which I am sure you remember. I am pretty sure that the famous flower he took to the funeral from the so-called Russian Lieutenant was just an excuse to be there – I am certain that it was not just sentimentality on his part. He was too good an operator for that."

The General agreed and decided it was time to order some coffee for the two of them. He was beginning to admire the style of Bortsov and wanted to chat longer with the man he had chosen for this important job after he had decided to fire the previous GRU chief who had sanctioned the now infamous Aldanov venture.

There was time for ten minutes of warm and informal updates about their families and colleagues until the General said it was time for his next meeting. "I look forward to our next briefing – so good luck," he said cheerfully as his protegee left.

Chapter 28

Tracking "Lou"

Whoever "Lou" really was, Ilia and Alina succeeded in working out his regular routines. Each morning, he would throw out his trash into a garden bin and then wait for an 8am pick-up by a lady who they assumed lived nearby and drove him to the city. There was obviously no easy way in which they could track what happened to him there, but he usually returned to his apartment by about 6pm, usually walking to this new address - either from a bus ride or from someone's car.

Then in the evening, he occasionally appeared in a tracksuit for a run through a pathway to a nearby park area. Then he would stop on the way back at the small shopping mall to order a soda to drink as he relaxed for ten minutes. On other evenings, he would go to the mall to buy groceries – but not more than he could comfortably carry on his way back. They had then observed him over just one weekend when he relaxed by mixing with neighbours as he drank coffee in one of the mall establishments, and then had a pizza in another. On the Sunday afternoon, he walked to the metro station and appeared to take a train into DC – but they were unable to follow him.

All this enabled them to develop a plan which the two agents presented to a meeting back at the Embassy with Kotov and Alexeyev.

"First, we will find a way to make some door-to-door marketing deliveries to the properties along the road one morning after he leaves for work," explained Ilia. "This will provide cover while one of us retrieves some items from his trash can. And of course we will have our small plastic bags and boxes with us."

The two chiefs agreed this was a good start as Ilia continued: "Then in the evening, and again at the weekend, either singly or together we will follow him discretely to discover which café he is using. Then between us, we can find a way to pick up items he has used such as a cup, napkin or plastic fork. We think he also has an occasional cigarette so there may be a fag-end we can collect as well".

Then Alina added: "One more thing, he does seem to use a lot of paper tissues when he goes running and to mop his brow when he relaxes with a drink afterwards so if we see a way to retrieve one of these, it could be the most important of all."

Kotov congratulated the two young agents on the successful first stage of their assignment but added that he was concerned about their anonymity after being seen around the area quite a few times. "It's a busy road," said Alina. "There are cars and people around all the time and I have never parked my car in the same place twice. Also, we have taken care to wear different clothes and hats each time – and I change my hair style, which I am sorry to say Ilia cannot do. But I have told him to shave off his beard before we go back again."

Alexeyev said he was also impressed by their report and went on to ask a series of questions about their approach to the next stage. But he seemed to be satisfied by their answers and then took them carefully through every detail of their plan to retrieve possible DNA samples.

Finally, Kotov nodded his agreement and gave them the go-ahead, adding: "But if you see any change in the man's movements which makes you think your presence may have been spotted, do not persist until we have had a chance to rethink the plan. So good luck to you both and when you get your spoils, be sure to bring them back to Alexeyev immediately so that he can brief the laboratory team here and get them working on the comparisons – if they can successfully find any DNA samples."

The next morning, Ilia and Ilina set off early to Falls Church and watched from a safe distance as their target's colleague arrived on time and set off for their day at Langley. Next the two Russian agents went into the food store in the mall and found a display box containing a pile of colourful leaflets promoting a new brand of detergent – and each of them took a dozen or so copies. Then they started their planned deliveries to letterboxes along the road nearest to the apartment block and choosing their moment carefully, Ilia went to the trash bin they saw being used by their target and slipped on a pair of rubber gloves before picking out selected items to put into the plastic bags in his pocket. With the first mission completed they quickly drove away and returned to the embassy in the city and handed over the plastic bags to Alexeyev.

"That's the first instalment," said Ilia. "And we will go back this evening and see where mister Lou goes – probably running if it is still a fine evening."

And that was exactly what they saw soon after his return to the apartment. They waited within sight of the usual café and he was obviously a creature of habit because after about 30 minutes, he returned hot and breathless to sit at an outside table with his plastic cup of soda. He did not smoke, but Ilia had moved quietly inside the cafe alone to order a coke and he was surprised to see that after wiping his mouth with a paper napkin, Lou stuffed the napkin into his empty cup and then jogged away towards his home. The café staff were too busy to notice his departure, so Ilia quickly went outside, sat at the same table and neatly squeezed the cup and napkin into a bag from his pocket. He then relaxed with his coke until he was joined by Ilina who had watched the slick manoeuvre with admiration.

"That napkin could be the clincher," she suggested, and they both had another drink as they relaxed for a while before driving back to the embassy. On the way, she called her chief and told him to stand by for another piece of evidence. He waited for their arrival and after hearing their story, he took their plastic bag off to the laboratory after telling them they might just have an answer the next morning.

Chapter 29

The Swap

The 'back channel' contacts between the British Foreign Office and their counterparts in Moscow were already vibrating. In their carefully worded exchanges, London wanted to know what was the real story behind the detention of Lady Briggs? What had she done to lead them to this unusual action against the wife of a business visitor? After their expected explanation about secret recordings of her conversations, there came the hint of an admission from the Russians that they did not yet have any firm evidence yet to support charges being brought against her.

Reading between the lines, the experts in London could recognise that there was another motive behind this arrest. In a carefully-worded message, they asked the Russians what it would need for them to allow Lady Briggs to move from her cell into a guarded apartment, as the British embassy lawyer had requested. It worked! After two days of silence the reply came back suggesting that the British could also consider the early release from prison of their diplomat Yakov Rozovsky.

"Aha – that's it, of course" was the reaction in the depths of Whitehall. And the information was discretely passed to the decision-makers upstairs.

By then, the media furore over the detention of Lady Briggs had reached fever pitch and the Bitish government was finding it a major distraction. The Prime Minister asked for a report from the Foreign Secretary on the matter and then at a meeting which followed, he asked what would be the downside of releasing the Russian diplomat?

The Foreign Secretary told him: "At the time, we needed to give a strong answer to the blatant Ricin attack by the GRU agents in Portsmouth. But he is a relatively low level official and he has served over two years of his eight year sentence. He was recently moved to an open prison where he is counting the days while the Russian embassy continues their legal case against the length of his sentence".

The Prime Minister thought carefully about the options before deciding his response. "This woman and her ballerina friends in Moscow have made a good story, but there is nothing else in it, is there?" he asked. Getting a negative response, he then told his Foreign Secretary: "Then go ahead with one of those exchange jobs as quietly as you can. Just a straightforward statement later on to emphasise that the Russian has served a substantial part of his sentence. This should close it down and it will all be forgotten in a couple of weeks."

In Moscow, word had already come down to the Police Commissioner from the lawyers in the Home Affairs Ministry that Lady Briggs could be transferred to the guarded apartment as requested by the British embassy's lawyer, Sergei Oblomov. For three days, she had faced lengthy and intensive questioning for an hour or more by a Russian lawyer with an interpreter. But she had no information that could be useful to them, other than to confirm the names of the friends she had met. Also, Oblomov and Robin Charters had been allowed to visite her police cell for the permitted ten minutes, twice each day, and found that she was holding up well in the strange circumstances. She was comforted by the news that they were speaking to her husband every day and passing on his love and messages. But she was surprised to hear that he was back in England and they carefully explained that this was in her best interests so that he could work with the British authorities on securing her release.

Then on the fourth morning Oblomov arrived at the usual time, but with good news. She could hardly believe it when he told her: "The authorities here have agreed with our suggestion to move you out of here while they continue their inquiries. So today, you will be able to go into a small apartment near the British embassy. They will take you in a police car and Robin will meet you there to open the apartment and hand over the key to a police guard".

She took his hand and was staring to cry as she told him: "This is wonderful – thank you so much for getting me out of this place. I have been trying very hard not to make any more problems, but I have been close to giving up hope here."

"I am afraid it is not over yet," explained the lawyer, who added that he would now remain with her at the police centre until the move took place. "You will be under house arrest at the apartment with a permanent police guard and maybe some more questioning. But at least it will be more comfortable and we can still have our daily visits to let you know what is going on."

They did not have long to wait. Oblomov went outside to make some calls and after about 15 minutes, he returned with two armed officers and persuaded them that handcuffs would not be necessary as they escorted the lady out to a waiting car. The lawyer walked with them and when he was sure they were out of range of listening devices, he whispered to Lady Briggs: "This may not be for very long – I hear that the Brits are making some progress behind the scenes about your release."

As the car sped away, Oblomov called the Embassy with the news that they were on the way.

It was just two days later when Robin Charters was able to meet her at the flat to tell say that she was "almost free" – her seven-days ordeal in the hands of the Russian police had come to an end. It was 8am and the armed guard was watching closely as they walked out with her few possessions to a waiting embassy car. As they drove away, she could see that the two suitcases which she and her husband had brough to Moscow were already in the front of the vehicle as Robin explained that they were also being closely escorted by a Russian vehicle with two GRU officials who would ensure that they completed their part of the transaction for her release.

"You are part of what we call a spy swap," explained her British embassy escort, "And we are heading to a military airport and a Russian plane to take us from there to a neutral country for the official transaction to be completed."

Still bewildered by the unexpected events, Lady Briggs asked: "Is there somewhere I can freshen up before I meet anyone else. I have not really woken up yet and only had time for a cup of warm coffee when the guard came to rouse me this morning."

"I am so sorry," replied Robin. "Just hang on a bit longer and we will take good care of you. But we have to stick to the rules here until the Russians are confident that the British government has kept our part of the bargain."

"Did you say just now that it was a spy swap?" she asked quizzingly. "I am not being treated as a spy, am I?"

"No, don't worry," came the reply with a cheerful laugh. "It is just shorthand for the performance we have to go through. In fact, we have done this quite often and it happens when the two sides find it useful to get the release of their people for various reasons. I can assure you that no-one on our side will ever use the word spy in your case. Just try to relax for the next hour or so and all will be well."

Annelise Briggs decided that anything would be better than the police cell, and at least she had enjoyed two nights of more comfortable sleep in the embassy flat. From the nearby military airport, she and Robin flew in a small Russian aircraft accompanied by two serious-looking Russian officials. They said little until Robin told her quietly that they were actually landing in a small airfield in Finland. The group disembarked and in a small office building, she watched as documents were exchanged by the two Russians with a waiting group of three men – Robin explained quietly that they were two officials from the British Foreign Office plus their detainee who was a Russian diplomat. When the formalities were completed, he whispered "good luck" in her ear and told her it was time to walk across the room to the join the British group – and at the same time, their third man came forward and the two key participants crossed in the centre of the room without glancing at each other.

The "swap" was completed and Annelise was quickly taken outside to a small RAF aircraft with eight passenger seats which was parked a few dozen yards away. She was directed to a seat at the front, and her escorts took the seats behind her. Hardly a word was said until they had fixed their seat-belts, the engines had been started and the plane taxied out to the runway to take off. Then one of the British officials leaned forward and said: "Welcome back, Lady Briggs. It all worked smoothly as planned and we are on our way to an airport near London. My name is Nigel and this is Owen and we work in the Foreign Office – and by the way, there is someone else waiting to see you at the back of the aircraft."

The aircraft was accelerating noisily on the runway as she turned her head and she was amazed to see her husband, Richard, belted into one of the rear seats and blowing a kiss in her direction.

Chapter 30

Back in Moscow

Yazov Rozovsky had been surprised when a prison officer found him reading quietly in the garden of the 'open prison' in the English countryside and told him to come at once to the governor's office. When he got there, he found the governor was there with an official he knew from the Russian embassy in London who greeted him warmly with the news: "You are going home tomorrow."

This came as a shock to Rozovsky who had prepared himself for at least two more years in the relatively relaxed atmosphere of the prison before he would be considered for parole. He asked what had happened and was told in Russian – which the governor clearly did not understand – that he had just been told that Rozovsky been the subject of an exchange with a British woman being held on suspicion of espionage in Moscow.

"I'm sorry, but I don't know any more of the details," he continued. "I am just pleased to be able to bring you this news. My mission today is simply to tell you to be ready tomorrow morning at 9am when I will be here again with an officer from the British foreign office to collect you and your belongings. Apparently, we will be going to an airport where a plane will be waiting to fly you out of the country – and that is all I know."

"You mean I will be free?" asked the Russian, questioningly and still hardly believing the words he was hearing.

The prison governor intervened to emphasise that Rozovsky was still in detention until he was formally handed over to the Russians, with all the correct paperwork completed. "I will be here tomorrow to oversee the process and to ensure that it all goes as planned," he added, with appropriate authority in his voice.

After a restless night attempting to persuade himself that this was not all a dream, Rozovsky was helped by a warder to gather his belongings from his prison room and from the store where other confiscated possessions were kept. There was just time for a quick breakfast in the canteen before going to the governor's office again just before 9am. His former colleague from the London embassy was there together with a British government official who handed the formal release documents to the governor, who read them carefully and then told Rozovsky he was free to go.

Rozovsky then began to believe it was really happening as the three of them went to a waiting car which was then closely followed by a police motor cyclist as their escort for the 20-minutes drive to Gatwick airport. At the VIP terminal building, another more senior British official took over and after again checking the documents, the Russian diplomat said 'goodbye and good luck' to his former colleague as Rozovsky boarded a small, RAF jet aircraft together with the two British officials. "Where are we going?" asked Rozovky in his best English as the plane took off. "Finland," was the brusque reply and little more was said during the 2-hours flight other than a few words as they were served hot coffee and chocolate bars by the only crew member apart from the pilot and co-pilot.

On their arrival, Rozovsky was pleased that his belongings included a warm anorak jacket as they briefly encountered the Arctic air. Then in a small airport building, it seemed to him to be a short and efficient process between the two sets of officials before he was welcomed with bear hugs by two Russians who quickly escorted him out to another waiting plane which would take him to Moscow.

During the flight, he learned that one of them was from the foreign affairs department and the other from the defence ministry. They told him that they had done this sort of operation several times and they went on to talk freely to their latest charge to update him on the latest news ranging from politics to sport and the weather forecast. Rozovsky was excited to hear that his wife and family would be waiting to greet him on their arrival at the military airport near Moscow, as well as a government minister. It was a brief but heart-warming occasion and he was pleased to be told that he would be allowed to have a week at home to settle back into his family life after two years – and he was handed an official letter with details of where he should report for duty on the next Monday morning.

Fully refreshed, he duly arrived at the appointed office in the Ministry of Defence building to find the Deputy Minister, General Yazov awaiting his arrival together with Yuri Bortsov, Director of the GRU intelligence service. They both gave him a cordial welcome and the General commented on how well he looked after two years of incarceration in a British jail. Rosovsky explained that in the British system, well-behaved prisoners were rewarded with a transfer to what were called 'open prisons' after a year in a prison block. He then had to explain this system more fully, since it was something quite new to those more familiar with Russian practices. The General finally laughed about it and commented: "It would never work here – our prison staff would be killed in their beds."

Turning to business, the General began discussing Yakovky's future and told him: "You had a couple of years in the GRU section here before we moved you to London to give you some wider experience and you were in charge of the intelligence team there. So we are thinking about offering you the number two position under Yuri at the GRU headquarters – you know of course that Yuri has taken over there while you have been overseas - but we do have a few questions to sort out first."

Bortsov took over the lead in the discussion and it was clearly becoming more serious in the minds of the two senior men. Rosovsky could not begin to imagine what was coming next? That was until the GRU director looked him in the eyes and said sternly: "What was that red rose business all about? It made news headlines, it made us look ridiculous and the top people in Kremlin asked for an explanation. This stunt got you arrested and sent to prison for eight years. Whatever were you thinking about?"

Rosovsky took a deep breath and decided quickly that his best option was to hit back.

"I thought you knew my record better than to think I would do what you called a stunt," he began, firmly. "It was not a sentimental gesture at all, but I made it look like one to provide cover for my real objective. And as you well know, there was no way in which I could report back afterwards."

He went on to recall in detail what had occurred under Bortsov's predecessor at GRU who had approved Aldanov's secret mission to follow up his on-line contact with a woman working for the British navy in Portsmouth, UK. However, in the interests of secrecy, the plan had not been shared with anyone at the Russian embassy in London.

"But I had excellent contacts, as you would expect", continued Rosovsky. "And I heard about the plan several days before Aldanov arrived and I even knew that the MI5 in London were aware of the plan. So I kept my ear to the ground after the press started to publish headlines about the so-called Russian Lieutenant's date in the dockyard and then his arrest and court appearance. And then Moscow asked me to keep an eye on developments and told me to put my team on the trail of the woman called Marina Peters and to find a way to prevent her from giving evidence at the trial of Aldanov. And I am sure you both know the rest of the story."

The minister and the GRU chief looked at each other and it was General Yazov who commented. "I think you know more than we do and it seems as though that was another error by Bortsov's predecessor not to keep you informed. So I am sorry if we jumped to conclusions. Tell us what happened next about the funeral?"

Rosovsky went on to describe how the search for the woman drew a blank and they assumed she had been taken to a secret location until the trial. The agents had located her apartment in Portsmouth and with the agreement of Moscow, he had authorised them to leave a Ricin poison package in her mailbox as a last resort to achieve their objective. But then here was a surprise development which the General said he knew all about – the decision to bring Aldanov back to Moscow in a spy-swap so that there would be no trial.

"Again, this decision was not shared with me in London," said Rosovsky. "It all happened very quickly and the woman was back in her apartment before I knew. Then the Ricin poisoning story hit the headlines … and it brought back all the details of the Russian Lieutenant again. I took an immediate action to fly the two agents responsible back on the next flight to Moscow before they were implicated. We refused to make any comments and the Ambassador dealt with the press while I used my local contacts to discover what was happening at the local hospital where the woman had been taken. It became confusing when the hospital and the police announced that Marina Peters had died as a result of Ricin poisoning. Then a day later another informant told me about a mysterious ambulance departure from the at night to an airfield where a medivac plan was waiting".

Rosovsky said he tried but failed to connect these incidents but he added that the media were working at fever pitch, interviewing the woman's parents and friends and the local police. He went on to describe the coverage of the inquest which concluded that Marina Peters had been "murdered by person or persons unknown". Then came the announcement of the funeral arrangements.

"By then", he continued, as the two senior officials listened intently, "I was hearing rumours that the death of the woman had been faked and one of my contacts actually knew a staff member at the local funeral company who said there was something odd about the funeral and cremation plans. They were not being made by the family as usual, but by someone senior in the navy and the company's boss was handling all the arrangements personally.

"And finally, I heard that a member of the woman's family was questioning the plan for the ashes of Marina Peters to be scattered in the sea on the same day as the funeral service. And so I decided to go to the ceremony with my red rose so that I could mix with the mourners and try to discover more. But I was arrested for being an accessory to murder and went to jail. And that is the background to what you called a stunt, sir," concluded Rosovsky, firmly.

"Quite a story," commented the general and Bortsov added: "You did good job and I am sorry that nobody knew."

The next day, Rosovsky's appointment as deputy director of the GRU was announced

Chapter 31

A Perfect Match!

The DNA sample was tested during the evening by the laboratory specialist at the Russian embassy in Washington – and it was a positive. It matched the details on the personal information chart for Nikolai Aldanov provided by Moscow and the report went immediately to Yuri Kotov when he arrived at the embassy the next morning. He decided to break the good news to his team and to the Ambassador and set up a meeting for 9.15am.

When Ilia and Alina arrived for their regular morning meeting in the office being used by Kotov, he greeted them cheerfully to tell them: "You are just in time. We have to go to a meeting with the Ambassador in a few minutes."

As they walked across the courtyard in a morning rain shower, Kotov said: "Don't' worry, the sun will be shining for you soon." They settled round the conference table in the richly furnished office and after their greeting from the top man, Kotov began: "I have some great news to share with you, sir - and with my two young colleagues here. As you know, they have been trying to identify one of our suspects who may be the wanted man Aldanov. Well, they eventually secured some DNA samples yesterday and our lab here identified them last night as being a perfect match. So may I say well done to you both – Lou Welensky is our man."

"My congratulations to you all," added the Ambassador. "So what is the plan now?"

Kotov went on to describe in detail how the two agents had followed up information from a local informer which had put them on the trail of a recent newcomer to the Falls Church area. He appeared to have a Russian background and his name was Lou Welensky. They had discovered the apartment where he had just moved in and saw that he was sometimes given a lift in the morning by a woman who lived nearby and they believed she worked at the CIA headquarters in Langley. He went on to describe how they had patiently and discretely followed his movements each evening over a two weeks period and had been able to create the pattern of his domestic activities.

The Ambassador showed his appreciation of their efforts and asked Ilia: "After watching this man for a while, do you believe that this is the same man you knew in Tokyo?"

"Yes, I do sir," came the confident reply. "Even before we found the DNA samples, I could recognise the way he walked and behaved in the shops and restaurants. I felt pretty sure that behind the beard was the man I knew as Aldanov."

Kotov picked up the story and continued: "Our job now is to keep him under surveillance while we work out our plan of action. As you know, Ambassador, our instructions from Moscow are to confirm his identity and then to report that we have eliminated him as a traitor. And we have several different options to consider, as you know. How do you think the CIA and maybe the media will react to the news of his disappearance?"

"We just want the Americans to know that we take it seriously when they detain one of our diplomats overseas and then bring him back here to be an informant," said the Ambassador. "We must respond accordingly."

The two young agents listened intently and indicated that they understood the Ambassador's instructions and Ilia offered his suggestion: "Our man seems to walk out alone to the nearby park as well as the food store and coffee shop most evenings so he is quite vulnerable – but of course there are usually other people around all the time."

Alina wanted to be involved too and added: "I have also heard about the use of various poisons which could be used at his apartment – I read about the use of Novichoc in the UK which went a bit wrong, but we could be more careful."

"Thanks for your ideas, but I think poisoning might be a bit difficult in an apartment block and we cannot risk getting the wrong person again," said the Ambassador. "I think a gunshot job is what we need, probably when he is walking or running in the park. Is it a location where a gunman could wait somewhere in hiding until the target appears?"

Ilia confirmed that there were enough trees and bushes in the park to provide cover and Kotov then asked the top man: "So do we have a trained shooter on our team here?"

"Well, we do have one or two. But I have another idea which would help to confuse the Americans," replied the Ambassador. "As you know, this country is awash with guns of all kinds and in parts of this city there are groups of criminals and drug dealers with shootings taking place nearly every day. My information network here can easily identify a gunman or two who will do anything for a few thousand dollars. What do you think?"

"I like it," said Kotov, thoughtfully. "But one of our people would need to be with the gunman to ensure that he did the job. How do you feel about that, Ilia?"

"No problem," came the quick reply.

Chapter 32

The Targets

Yuri Bortsov went to Yazov Rozovsky's office the next morning and apologised for the misunderstand at their meeting with the minister. "I am sorry we got it wrong," he continued. "But we are pleased that you explained things as you did. The reason we were so anxious to get you back from London is that the bosses at the Kremlin have followed your career closely and had you flagged for promotion – and I am pleased to have you here now as my deputy.

"The other reason, "He continued, "is that we have a major project in our plans for a big hit in the UK and you must have gained some good knowledge during your two years there at the Embassy in London."

Bortsov then explained the progress so far on his four targets which were dominating the work of the GRU. These, he said, were intended to restore the prestige of the department after a series of setbacks – one of which was the arrest and imprisonment of Rozovsky himself. The first challenge therefore, was to track down the former agent, Aldanov, who had been posted to Japan where he was abducted by the CIA and taken to the USA as an informer. The aim was to eliminate him as a traitor.

The second challenge was then to identify and detain a high profile British hostage who could be used In a spy-swap to secure the return of Rozovsky to Moscow – which of course had already succeeded

He went on to describe the third challenge which was to identify and deal with a mystery female CIA agent who had been involved in losing a valuable cyber operation in Canada and then a crucial informant with the US military in Japan.

"This is proving more difficult," continued Bortsov. "But we have some ideas and I will come back to that. The fourth project is where you come in because we intend to carry out a significant hit in the UK to show our real strength in the world of secret agencies. I want you to liaise with Igor Malenkov, who is now our man in London, and come up with a choice of two or three possible targets we can consider. Then I want you to go to London to us your experience in the implementation of our operation."

Rozovsky reassured his chief that he fully understood, adding that he was pleased to be back and appreciated the opportunity he had now been given as deputy chief of the GRU. "But what has happened to Kotov? I understood that he was number two here".

"His title is assistant director and I have sent him to the States to mastermind the current operation there – but your title is deputy director and therefore my right-hand man. Okay?" answered Bortsov.

The new deputy director agreed and said he appreciated the confidence being shown and added that he had some comments to contribute.

"First," he said. "I think it is unlikely that the British foreign office will grant a diplomatic visa to me so soon after my time in one of their prisons, so I may have to work with Malenkov at long distance. I know he is a competent operator and that should not be a problem. Secondly, if and when I do get there, I would like to follow up the contacts I made two years ago during the Aldanov business to see whether there is any new information about what I think was a fake funeral. I believe there will be a clue somewhere about your mystery CIA agent. But that will have to wait, so now can you give me some idea of the targets you have in mind for what you call a hit on facilities there?"

"You are right about the diplomatic visa issue of course," replied Bortsov. "But we have some good people in London and we can both work with them from here if necessary to get their input and then work together on the their follow-up plans."

He went on to ask for his deputy's view on the ideas he had so far about possible UK targets and outlined his idea about using remote-controlled drones to drop explosive devices on key locations which might not have top level security. As a hit on the USA, he had considered their air bases and communications centres in the UK but added that he thought these would be too well protected and instead he was now considering the residence of the US Ambassador in London' Regents Park area – "it might be more vulnerable than the embassy itself," he added. "And a survey by our observation satellites will tell us a lot more."

Rozovsky said he thought these were creative ideas, and his boss then went on to describe another UK target he had been studying. This was the Porton Down laboratory centre 100 miles from London which he believed to be an advanced research establishment for biological and chemical warfare.

"Even some minor damage there would be a huge psychological blow to the West and would demonstrate our ability to target such installations," he added. "But we would need to do some detailed research in advance on the best methodology – and by the way, this facility is in a rural area not far from the city of Salisbury and you will remember what happened there with our plan to find Sergei Skripal. And we don't want anything like that to happen again."

"That sounds really interesting – and has there been any progress in locating Skripal while I have been locked away?" was the question that followed. Told that there had been absolutely no information on this, Rozovsky suggested that he would also like to have another go at locating this Russian spy in due course when he could get back to the UK. But on the main issues of the day, it was agreed that he would spent time working with Malenkov to research these possible targets more fully and to consider various ways of carrying out meaningful hits.

"It's good to have you back, Yazov", he said, ending the meeting with a bear-hug. "You expertise is exactly what I was hoping for to carry out our new plans. Let me know how you are progressing and also whether you or Malenkov have any other suggestions."

During the following days, the two experienced GRU men prepared their plans in a series of confidential calls. These included securing aerial and space surveillance of the locations, the study of local area maps, and agreeing to have one of their trusted London-based agents carry out a search for nearby locations suitable for the discrete launching of drones. Then Rozovsky asked about the latest strike equipment, since he was "somewhat out of date." He was told that the latest development for this type of operation was the HIID – or high impact incendiary device – which was small and light enough to be carried by a radio-controlled drone.

"Do you have this equipment in London now," asked Rozovsky. "It might be a problem getting them to the UK at this time?"

"Don't worry," came the comforting reply. "Our technical guys here have managed to acquire all the component parts in various ways and they can assemble whatever we need when the time comes. And we know how to acquire drones there as well – they are available on-line to anyone."

Chapter 33

The Elimination!

The Washington Post front page headline shouted: *"MURDER IN FALLS CHURCH?"* and then on the next line: *"Police say gun death may be murder or suicide".*

The report described how walkers in a Falls Church park heard a gunshot at dusk on the previous evening and then found a man lying at the side of a footpath with a head wound and a handgun nearby. They called the police who were quickly on the scene, followed by officers from the FBI, and the area was quickly roped off as a crime scene.

One local resident, Michael Edison, told a Post reporter: "These things just don't happen in this part of Washington. I was walking my dog and it was a fairly quiet evening until there was the sound of a single gunshot which alarmed my dog. I ran towards the area where the sound appeared to come from and two or three other people came from different directions. We saw this man lying on the verge alongside the footpath. He was bleeding from a head wound and he was clearly unconscious and there was a gun on the ground beside him. One of the other people dialled the emergency number and reported what we had discovered. Several more people arrived on the scene and we tried to keep them away from the area until we heard the sirens of the police and ambulance services.

"The medical people were there first and seemed to confirm that there was little they could do as about four or five uniformed officers from the Virginia state police roped off the area and started to take statements from those of us who were there – not that we could tell them very much. They asked all of us if we lived locally and if we saw anyone who appeared to be a stranger. I certainly didn't."

The Washington Post report continued with a statement issued by the Fairfax County police HQ late at night which confirmed that they were investigating the death of a man discovered in Falls Church with a gunshot wound. It continued: "A handgun was found at the scene and investigations are focussed on discovering whether this was a case of suicide or possibly murder. A document carried by the victim provided a possibly identification and the inquiry is now being led by the FBI who will issue any further statements."

The early morning TV shows on all the local channels led on this new breaking story, with correspondents reporting live from the Falls Church park. There had been a tip-off to the press that the CIA was also involved in the inquiries and there were also TV cameras at the gates to the agency's headquarters. But with no further facts or statements to use, even the most intrepid reporters could only speculate and use the evocative initials "CIA" as often as possible, together with the phrase "possible murder". Those in Falls Church interviewed several residents who heard the gunshot and a few who went to the scene. Some of them knew that several CIA employees lived in the area, but none could provide any specific information.

Meanwhile, the FBI investigators discovered that there were no usable fingerprints on the gun, which had only been fired once. This indicated that it had been wiped clean before it was left near the body and this, together with the type of gun, indicated a "professional shooting". Also, the post mortem had indicated that the location of the single head wound was not consistent with a suicide case and the bullet retrieved from the skull was a type commonly used by street gangs and was probably fired by a trained assassin.

When this assessment reached Larry Atkins, the chief FBI investigator in Washington DC, he had already spoken to Bob Smithers, the Operations Director at the CIA headquarters, who said he had heard the shocking news on the radio. He was able to confirm the name Louis Welensky found on the victim was known to them but that the CIA had no past history of the man which could be related to this tragic occurrence. But when his caller went on to say that his might actually be a case of murder, he realised that this was likely to be a much more complicated inquiry with a good deal of media interest. He then told the FBI official that he would liaise with the CIA's investigation branch as well as the information department and would share the relevant names with him for any further developments.

Smithers could only shout to himself: "Jesus Christ!" as he put the phone down. Then he called to arrange an urgent meeting with the CIA chief upstairs. He had also heard the radio news about the shooting incident but was even more alarmed when Bob Smithers told him: "It's that Aldanov man again – he gets

177

into trouble everywhere – in England, in Japan and now here in Falls Church. But at least he is dead this time."

"But he was really useful in his de-briefing here, I think, so your operation to get him here was really worthwhile. Don't be hard on yourself, Bob," said the top man. "Let's stay shtum so far as possible and see how it all develops."

Later in the day, the FBI and the Fairfax County police eventually issued a joint press statement:

"At about 7pm yesterday. we received a call to report a gunshot in the Falls Church park at about 7pm and officers found the body of man with a head injury and a handgun was beside him. When medical teams arrived the man was pronounced dead and our enquiries led to his identification as Louis Welensky with an address in a nearby apartment block. An identity check confirmed that he had a Russian background and had been in contact with the CIA at their headquarters in Langley, Virginia. No witnesses to the incident have been discovered, but neighbours who had arrived quickly on the scene have provided statements. They did not see any other people or strangers in the area.

This incident was regarded as a suspected suicide pending further investigations, but the post mortem indicated that there was another party involved and this has now become a murder inquiry. The park has been closed so that a detailed search of the area can be made for any evidence. There will be a further statement and a news conference later."

At the Russian Embassy, the GRU group watched the story unfolding on local TV and Yuri Kotov turned to Ilia and said: "Well done – you obviously got the right man. It all seemed to work just as planned and I assume you gave the envelope to the mysterious gunman?"

"Yes, and I don't even know his name," replied Ilia, enjoying the moment. "I met him twice, exactly as arranged by our contact, at two different places in the nearby shopping centre. On the first evening, we did a recce in the park and he identified a couple of concealed places with a good view of the footpath and we watched the timing of our target's evening run. There seemed to be fewer people around on the second evening and so the gunman found his spot and we waited. He was a real pro – and said very little. But he was no more than five yards from the target when he fired the one shot. He was wearing gloves of course and quickly placed his gun by the body and then came back and just asked me 'is that OK?' He took the envelope from me without even checking the contents and just disappeared into the woodlands without another word.

"I could hear people approaching and so I went off quickly in the opposite direction and then heard the sirens from the emergency services about five minutes later. I just took the metro and went back to the hotel in Georgetown for a stiff drink of whisky before sending you my 'job done' text. You replied 'see you in the morning' And here I am".

The small group all said 'well done' and then Yuri Kotov added a word of caution to Ilia: "We will arrange for you to stay here inside the embassy compound for a few days. It is unlikely that the police will track down the gunman, but just in case, we have to remember that if he was able to identify you, they could regard you as an accessory to murder. No-one here even knows who the gunman was. Our under-cover man in DC was the fixer and he is too smart to leave any trail, so I think we should be safe."

Kotov then went to report the situation to the Ambassador, who was pleased to be able to send a brief message to his liaison minister in the foreign affairs department in Moscow, and to Yuri Bortsov in the GRU headquarters: "The traitor has been eliminated."

Chapter 34

Finding Launch Sites

A UK foreign office media relations official was at the Northolt airport near London when the RAF plane arrived and he went on board to welcome Lady Briggs, together with her husband. He then surprised them with the news that there would be a news conference on the tarmac as they disembarked. He had to persuade a reluctant Annelise that she should appear in her present dishevelled appearance. And as intended, the questions were all about how she had been treated by the Russians and she duly described her detention in the police cell in detail. "It was a ghastly experience and I had no idea what I was supposed to have done," she said in answer to a bombardment of questions from the press and TV reporters.

But after just a few minutes, the government official intervened and said that there would be a further news conference in a day or two – "when Lady Briggs has had an opportunity to recover from her ordeal". And he quickly whisked the couple away by car to their home in Surrey.

It had been enough for the TV news channels and the press to headline the story of a "ghastly experience", together with unladylike shots of Annelise with Lord Briggs as they stood by the aircraft. This coverage overwhelmed reports about the Russian diplomat who had been released to secure the secret 'swap'.

It was the next afternoon when the official news conference was arranged at the elegant home of Lord and Lady Briggs near Haslemere. The Foreign Secretary himself was there to offer the government's appreciation of "the dignified way in which Annelise had handled her illegal detention in Moscow". He confirmed that formal protests had been lodged with the Russian Government and that there would be further measures including the restriction of visas for diplomats and financial embargos on investments in the UK. He dismissed a question about the 'swap' as being insignificant – "the man had served most of his prison term anyway" was all that he would say.

Meanwhile, in the basement level rooms of the Russian Embassy in London, there was feverish activity as the technical team assembled two HIID bombs and two drones for the proposed key missions. Also, the newly-arrived agent Egerov was briefed and then sent to visit Wiltshire and to check the area around the Porton Down research laboratories. Malenkov himself spent time familiarising himself with the Regents Park area and specifically the gated entrance to the ambassadorial residence, proudly flying its stars and stripes flag.

The team reconvened a few days later, together with maps and arial photographs, to consider their options. The deputy GRU chief Rozovsky joined them on the confidential line from Moscow and they heard first the report from the agent who carried out the Porton Down research. The photos showed a group of six large low level buildings in a fenced area with just one gated entrance. The campus was surrounded by open Salisbury Plain farmland and there were also details of two small villages within a few miles of the site.

Then Egerov came up with a suggestion which got the attention of the group. "Setting up a launch site for a drone somewhere in the open countryside might actually be spotted, even at night," he began. "And I think it might be more discrete if we rented a holiday cottage in one of the nearby villages for a few days. They seem to be quite busy at holiday times and a couple or family with a 4-wheel drive vehicle or even a suitable camper van would seem to be quite normal there. After doing all the preparatory work and setting up the target data, our people could just drive the vehicle to a quiet spot in the night and then carry out the launch from the open doors at the back . What do you think?"

"Sounds like a good idea", said Malenkov and the group went on to examine the idea in greater detail. They agreed that a typical holiday couple or family would be needed for the cottage rental to avoid any suspicion in the neighbourhood. As they considered possible candidates among the embassy staff, one strong possibility emerged – there was a woman agent in the GRU team whose partner was an attache on the Ambassador's staff. They had been in the UK long enough to be reasonably fluent English speakers and they had past experience of vacations in the UK. It was noted that they would need to inform the UK authorities about their plans to travel outside the London area – "but they have done this before and might not be subject to close surveillance if they were seen to be just touring in the West of England in a camper van," observed the bureau chief.

From Moscow, Yuri Rozovsky applauded the progress they were making and the meeting agreed to consider this idea, but ruled out the idea of renting a cottage in a nearby village – "which could leave evidence behind". They moved on to start planning the details and asked if the couple would have the technical skills to launch and activate the drone. But one of the group knew that their fellow agent, who they all knew as "W", was a very bright lady and her partner was a computer nerd, so they could quickly learn what was necessary?

Turning to the second operation, Malenkov said he thought the US Ambassador's house was vulnerable, but that finding a suitably remote launch location in the middle of London was the major problem. The closest park area seemed full of people at all times, but he had noted several tall buildings within a range of the target which might offer a suitable rooftop, but more research was clearly needed. Then there was the problem of conveying a drone and its attachment unobtrusively to the chosen spot.

In conclusion, Rozovsky again complimented the group and told them: "I have heard enough now to prepare a report to the Director which he will need to run past the defence minister before we get the go ahead. But I still think we need some more ingenuity to succeed with these operations."

Details of the plan were shared with Yuri Bortsov who gave it his approval and then he sent an outline with his "recommendation to proceed" to his minister at the department of defence. It was then reviewed by the Kremlin and the reply came back promptly: "Go ahead – and synchronise the two attacks for maximum effect".

Chapter 35

COBRA is convened

It was 2am on a Monday morning when the Commissioner of London's Metropolitan Police Force was woken at home by a call on his emergency phone. It was the London Fire Brigade chief with news of an incident at Winfield House in Regents Park: "At the moment, I can only tell you that there was an explosion and a fire about 15 minutes ago and we have several units there. I will update you as soon as I get any feedback."

Commissioner Charles Winstanley instantly knew that this was the home of the US Ambassador to Britain and therefore of crucial importance and he quickly called the emergency number for the police chief of the London area which included Regents Park to ask for more information. "Yes, sir", he replied, recognising the voice instantly. "I am actually gathering details now from my response team who are there so can you stay on the line for just a moment?"

He was back on the line within two minutes to report that it appeared to be caused by an external device of some kind which had struck one wing of the house, which was now on fire and that there were believed to be some casualties. He added that all available emergency services had been called to the scene.

The police Commissioner quickly gathered his senses, dressed and without waiting to call his driver, he drove in his own car from his suburban home through the quiet London streets to Scotland Yard and was in the operations centre within 10 minutes. He was reviewing the initial information and watching an alarming video feed from the fire service when he had another call, this time from Caroline Svenson, the deputy head of the Security Services, MI5, who was on weekend duty. "What's going on Charles?" she began. "I was just seeing a first report of a fire at Winfield House when I had an urgent call from the Wiltshire police to say that they are following up reports of some sort of fire at the Porton Down laboratories. One incident like this might well be accident. Two at this time of night make me think of terrorism, so I am alerting the key government officials."

Commissioner Winstanley said he agreed and told his caller that he was already in the Met's operations centre and would keep her informed.

From Winfield House came the news that the Ambassador and his wife were safe and unharmed and had been moved to the secure US embassy building two miles away south of the Thames. However, two members of their housekeeping staff who had been sleeping in the West wing had been rescued from the burning building and taken by ambulance to Charing Cross hospital with serious injuries. Meanwhile the fire service teams had prevented the fire spreading to the main part of the building and they had discovered what appeared to be the remains of an incendiary device. Army bomb experts had been called and were already on their way to the location.

Caroline called again from MI5 said she now had her chief "M" on the line and he wanted to brief the Prime Minister's office at Number Ten as soon as possible, but first wanted he more information from Wiltshire. She said she had opened a line to the police chief in Salisbury who was on his way to Porton Down. She connected his call into Scotland Yard and told him to go ahead and update them both:

"It is not good," he began. "All the emergency services are there now and it seems that some sort of missile has hit one of the laboratory buildings. There were two staff working inside at the time and it contains hazardous materials of some kind. Several security officers on night duty went to the building at once and activated the alert system which they have all practised regularly. I now have the fire chief on another line and will get back to you in a few minutes."

"M" then said he had heard enough to be able to inform the Prime Minister's office. He made an urgent call and recommended a meeting as soon as possible of COBRA – the government's Civil Contingencies Committee, which meets when needed in the Cabinet Office Briefing Room. He also advised his Number-Ten contact to call the US embassy and include the US Ambassador in the meeting.

As more details came through from both locations, there was the news that the two staff scientists working in the Porton Down laboratory had been found by the security staff who had put on their Hazmat suits to enter the burning building. The emergency medical team had arrived by then and confirmed that both scientists were dead and also two of the rescuers had succumbed to dangerous fumes and were taken to hospital in

Salisbury. A wide area had been cordoned off and the fire service team in protective gear was still working to contain the damage to the one building.

"M" had just completed a preliminary briefing document for the Prime Minister when he had an unexpected update from the Ministry of Defence. The bomb disposal team sent to Winfield House had been able to identify the remains of the missile – and it was a Russian incendiary device. Also, it appeared to have been delivered by a drone manufactured in the UK.

The COBRA meeting assembled in Whitehall at 9am on a Monday morning, chaired by the Prime Minister together with the Home Secretary, the Foreign Secretary and the Defence Secretary who had all been rushed back from their weekend homes. Also there at the committee table was the US Ambassador, Henry Burbeck, with his security adviser, the Commissioner of the Metropolitan Police, "M" from MI5 and several advisers from government departments who were seated behind the principals. And before they began, "M" suggested that to remain up to date, they should add the Wiltshire police chief on the speaker phone.

The Prime Minister began the meeting by welcoming the participation of Chief Superintendant Jenkinson from his car at Porton Down – "We appreciate all that you and your team are doing there in this dreadful situation and we will hear an update from you in a few minutes."

He then greeted the US Ambassador and sympathised with him for the damage they had been seeing to his residence, and then continued:

"It seems that what at first looked like a resumption of terrorism here is in fact something even more serious. This now appears to be a co-ordinated Russian attack on two strategic targets here in the UK but intended to hit the USA as well. They may appear limited in scale, but the message from the Kremlin is clear and we must respond accordingly. Let me ask our friend from MI5 to tell us any background he knows about?"

"M" then described how these two actions had clearly been the work of the Russian secret services and carried out from the London embassy without involving military resources. However, it was probably relevant that MI6's international sources had been monitoring increased military activity in Russia with their troops moving south towards Ukraine and carrying out joint exercises with Belarus. They had also monitored recent statements which indicated a more aggressive attitude developing towards the West and NATO. He then added that he knew that the CIA had been recognising the same changes and the US Ambassador said that he could confirm this, and he knew from their sources in Russia that the Kremlin was sounding more belligerent every day.

The Prime Minister said he fully understood this update and interrupted the discussion to ask: "If you are still there Jenkinson, any further news from Wiltshire?"

"Thank you, sir," came a confident reply. "I am honoured to be part of this important meeting, but I cannot give you any good news. We now have three deaths here as a result of the attack and although the fire has been contained, there is a serious issue with fumes from the building which apparently housed a quantity of stored material which is extremely toxic. Fortunately,

189

there is no housing nearby. The Director of Porton Down has now arrived here and he is advising the fire service team who have succeeded in preventing the fire spreading beyond just two of the buildings. But it will all take time before we can allow the military explosives team to search the rubble here".

"That sounds sensible," said the PM. "But the similarity between these two events leads me to assume that this is all the work of the same GRU team. We will immediately send a message to the Russian embassy telling them that we have evidence that these two serious incidents on British soil were caused by Russian actions and that we are lodging an official protest".

The US Ambassador said his President would also want to send a similar message to Moscow and that he would emphasise that the response to such a wanton action would have the support of NATO.

The Prime Minister then told his Foreign Secretary to immediately insist that the Russian Ambassador should come to the Foreign Office that day to receive the formal letter and to be told that the attacks would not go unanswered. Then turning to "M", he asked: "By the way, did you say in your report that the drone thing was British?"

"Yes sir, they are available to buy on-line here in various shapes and sizes, together with operating instructions," came the reply. "You may have heard that they have been something of a nuisance around airports and other places here for some time, by the way. And I am told that it would not be difficult for an expert to attach a small incendiary bomb device to one of them, direct it to a target and then crash it to do the damage."

The Defence Secretary then asked the Prime Minister: "Should our answer to these brazen and deadly attacks also be some sort of reciprocal action. I can work on some suggestions?"

The PM nodded his agreement just as on the line from Wiltshire, the Chief Constable was able to interrupt the meeting with some new information. "Our traffic cameras and satellite images in the area have now identified recordings of a white camper van which was parked about a mile from Porton Down during the night," he reported. "Soon after the explosions were heard, the vehicle was seen driving off northwards in the early hours and we were able to circulate the registration number and description. And just a few minutes ago, I was informed that the vehicle has been traced to a car park at Bristol airport where the police have detained two men for driving offences. And I can also tell you that they have both been identified as Russians. I will let you know more later."

"Well done Wiltshire. I think that clinches it", said the PM, with his familiar ebullience.

He then continued the meeting by stressing that both targets had clearly been selected to make the maximum impact, regardless of civilian casualties and he asked the American ambassador to convey his concerns for everyone involved at Winfield House. He then instructed his staff to prepare a full press statement and to ensure that the media had as much access as possible to the damage at the two locations for photographs and TV camera crews – and to emphasise the situation regarding casualties.

He concluded: "It seems like the Kremlin is flexing its muscles. Let's all meet again at the end of the day, and then get the background assessments from the experts at the CIA and MI6".

Chapter 36

Tom and Mary

In the Intelligence Section of the America embassy in Tokyo, Samantha Lord was busy completing the paperwork for her debriefing meetings following the departure of the CIA Director Bob Smithers together with the Russian Aldanov. She was helped by the local CIA chief, Melanie Mackintosh and other colleagues during several days of unfamiliar activity – but none of them knew about her next assignment, a wedding ceremony!

Her work was interrupted by three highly confidential messages.

The first was from Tom Spencer, brief and discretely worded, to say that he was back in London and working on plans which he would share with her later – and that he had been able to inform his boss and also Bob Smithers in the States in confidence about their future plans. He also asked her to confirm that she would be available in her Tokyo hotel room for an important phone call the next morning.

The second was from Bob Smithers in Washington: "Great stuff, Sam! You've scored a three-fer in just a few weeks – first tracking down the spy in Okinawa, second the capture of your Russian Lieutenant, and now our good friend Tom in London. Hearty congrats!"

The third was also from the CIA chief in Langley with copies addressed to Melanie Mackintosh and the US ambassador in Tokyo: "Following the successful completion of your assignment to Japan, your services are now required at HQ by the end of the month. Please make appropriate travel arrangements with the admin dept. and advise me of the date for your return. Suggest you fly via London with an overnight stopover for a meeting "tba" with the Deputy Operations Director in UK Intelligence Service. ."

Samantha found it hard to remain calm as she read these messages and it was helpful that the local CIA chief was at least in the picture so far as her travel plans were concerned.

"We shall be sorry to lose you so soon," said Melanie at their next meeting. "And that is a very helpful suggestion about flying to the States via London – it's so much easier than that long transpacific flight. I do it myself and you arrive in DC feeling much fresher after a break."

The travel conversation provided a useful distraction between business meetings, as Samantha waited longingly for that phone call the next morning. When it came, Tom was able to share more details about his plans and the timetable for the next few weeks. She was thrilled by his suggestion of a quiet wedding in Bermuda – and he said: "So glad you like the idea - that's great, so just leave it all to me". And when she told him that Bob Smithers had recalled her to Washington, and had suggested that she flew with a stopover in London he added: "Give me the details when you have them and I will fix a Heathrow hotel for us and we can dot a few i's and cross a few t's" .

The timetable was confirmed in the following days and their London reunion was romantic but all too short and when Samantha boarded her plane to Washington DC in the morning, she was glowing with happiness she had never experienced before.

Back at Langley, she found that Bob Smithers had already set the wheels in motion for the termination of her CIA engagement. "There are a few documents for you to sign and we have booked you a flight to Bermuda for next weekend, which is when Tom is due to fly there from London," he explained. "We will inform the team here that you have been reassigned and keep things low-key. But I would like you to come for a small farewell dinner at my home next Friday evening."

It was a hectic few days for Samantha, dealing with the formalities of her departure and also packing up her belongings at the apartment she shared with her CIA colleague. She noted that her travel documents for the flight to Bermuda were in the name of Samantha Lord and Bob explained that since she would be changing her name at the wedding, they had decided not to make yet another change. And when she told Tom Spencer about this in a phone call, he reassured her: "Don't' worry – you will always be Marina to me".

Then it was time to consider what to wear before taking a taxi to the Director's address, which was an impressive modern ranch-style home in the exclusive Potomac suburb of Washington. At the dinner with a group of senior colleagues and their wives, Bob paid tribute to the departing agent – "You have been a star," he said. "You arrived here after being an important and thankfully successful guinea pig for our medics to test a new antidote for

Ricin poisoning – you became a model case for our new identity team as we changed you from Marina into Samantha – then our trainers found you to be A1 throughout the tough course for new agents - and you went on to carry out successful assignments to Canada, Mexico and then Japan with real aptitude. What more could we ask – except that you stay with the Company a lot longer? But you have made the decision and you deserve to move on with your extraordinary life and so our good friend Tom Spencer is a very lucky man."

Before leaving the house, Marina found a quiet moment to ask her CIA chief: "By the way, what has happened to Aldanov?"

"Who?" replied Bob Smithers. "He doesn't exist any more so forget him."

She had learned enough about CIA confidentiality not to pursue the matter any further, but remained mystified as she said her farewells and went to complete her packing for her departure the next day.

Tom was already in Bermuda when his bride's plane arrived from Washington on the Sunday and at the elegant five-star Princess hotel, he told her about the plans he had made for a quiet wedding ceremony in the following week at the very British register office in Hamilton, the island's capital. She was impressed to her that the former CIA Director she knew as "M" - now retired and knighted as Sir Charles Bentley – had flown in for the occasion with his wife and were in a luxury suite in the same hotel.

Also in Bermuda for a one-week vacation in a nearby beachside apartment was Tom's younger brother Bernard and his wife

Marcia. Tom described how the two brothers were close, but very different careers meant that their relationship was usually a monthly phone call, unless some special family event occurred. The last of these had been the funeral in Scotland of their octogenerian father who had continued to manage their family home as a bed and breakfast for tourists in a small village in the foothills of the spectacular Highlands north of Aberdeen. His wife had passed away only two years earlier and he had since been helped in this B&B endeavour by Bernard and Marcia, who had found it a convenient opportunity to move into the large six-bedroomed former manse. It was also a good base for Bernard's work as a well-known wild-life and underwater cameraman, with a busy schedule of assignments for TV production companies.

It was after their father's funeral that Tom and Bernard had discovered that the house had been bequeathed to them jointly in the will. They had agreed that since Tom's life was firmly based in London, it would make good sense for the younger brother and his wife to move from their home in the Cotswolds to continue the business in Scotland. The brothers had quickly come to a mutually acceptable financial arrangement – and life went on until a phone call in which Tom told his surprised brother about the impending wedding.

"That's one thing I did not expect after all these years," was Bernard's reply. "But many congratulations – and who is the lucky lady?"

Tom went on to tell his brother only that Marina was in her late 30's but ready to settle down after a busy career working for the government in London and overseas. "I know you and Marcia will like her – she is a very warm and easy-going lady and we plan to spend our years together enjoying the Highlands like you," he added, before going on to describe the wedding plans, together with the date which was then just four weeks away.

"We will be there, of course", said Bernard. "And I know Bermuda quite well after doing three filming assignments there over the years. We even have our favourite digs on the island and a few local friends, so thanks for the date - I will get our plans fixed up. And by the way, where do you plan to live afterwards?"

"How about the Manse, at least at first," replied Tom. "We both want to get away from London life and after I sell my apartment in Primrose Hill, we would like to look around for somewhere in Scotland. Do you think that would work?"

"Yes, why not," said Bernard. "There is plenty of room and we don't really need the income or the work of running a B&B. I just didn't want to give up the business which dad had worked so hard to build up and we didn't want to turn away his regulars. They were all so fond of him and it was really nice to hear stories about him when we visited the Manse. Anyway, it will be even nicer to spend time together with you and your new wife."

It was a warm, sunny September day for the wedding and in the morning, the foursome met up for coffee on the terrace of the Princess Hotel. Bernard was an immediate 'hit' with Marina, who was intrigued by his stories of exploration in search of unusual wild-life in South America and under-water filming in the Arctic ocean. They were joined later by Sir Charles and Lady Bentley and it was soon time for the group tp drive off to the mid-day ceremony at the Register Office where the bridegroom's brother and his former boss were both equally impressed by Tom's uncharacteristic, loud and clear "I do" and then his warm embrace of Marina when the Registrar concluded the event with the familiar words – "You may kiss the bride."

Afterwards, the group celebrated back at the Princess Hotel – starting with champagne and followed by a lengthy, alcoholic lunch. As the conversation flowed, Sir Charles had been very reluctant to divulge many details about their work together, so Tom decided that he really had some explaining to do for his brother. He began to outline some of the more interesting experiences he could disclose about his career in the world of espionage.

"All I knew was that you were doing quite well as a boring civil servant," said an astonished and disbelieving Bernard. "Tell me more – if you can?"

"Can I just tell you that I did enough to get a gong when I retired," replied Tom and Sir Charles gently intervened and using his diplomatic skills, he turned to include the bride in the conversation. He and Lady Bentley were both impressed when Marina discretely answered their questions about how she came to meet her new husband – carefully leaving out the details of her Russian on-line date or her spell with the CIA. Then she told them in more detail the story of the dinner in Tokyo's finest geisha restaurant where Tom had 'popped the question'.

It was a memorable day for them all and over the next few days, the three couples were sad to be leaving the relaxing island of Bermuda for their respective flights back to the UK.

It was two weeks later when a furniture pantechnicon arrived at the Scottish manse from London, followed shortly the next day by Tom and Marina in his new, smart silver Lamborghini. Their arrival was watched with interest by some of the villagers and as the unloading went on around them, Bernard decided to invite a few local neighbours in for a welcome drink.

The two newcomers were introduced to his friends as Sir Tom and Lady Spencer – and Tom quickly intervened and told them: "We look forward to getting to know all our new friends here much better in the coming weeks – and please just call us Tom and Mary". He went to say how pleased they were to be among people they had heard so much about from Bernard and also from their parents before that.

Afterwards, an inquisitive Marina asked her new husband: "Where did Mary come from?"

"It's just to be more casual for the locals here," came the explanation, and Marina did not fully understand until Tom added: "I think it will also reduce the chances of someone remembering those days when the name of Marina was in the headlines. I don't think we want that dragged up in the press again, or we may have to move to somewhere even quieter – but you will always be Marina to me."

It was near the end of the tourist season and Bernard and Marcia had already decided not to accept any new bookings at The Manse until the newcomers had settled in and made some longer-term plans together. Over the next few days, the two couples made the necessary domestic changes and then Bernard told his brother that he was about to depart on a four-weeks filming assignment in Iceland. He added that it was such an interesting location that Marcia would be travelling with him. He then added casually that this would also give Tom and Marina some time together as newly-weds.

It proved to be a good opportunity for them to relax, make new friends and to explore the village and the wider area in the autumnal weather. They climbed the nearby mountains and began to feel "at home" in Scotland. They also made special efforts to become involved in some of the local activities. These included joining in for a convivial quiz night at the pub when Tom bought his round for everyone and modestly ensured that he and Mary did not win the prize money!

Chapter 37

One More Mission

Yakov Rozovsky was still deskbound at the GUR headquarters in Moscow, unable to travel back to London as he had hoped because the British embassy would not provide a diplomatic passport to a man who had been convicted by the court. But he still had one more target in mind – the MI5 chief who he had shadowed in his previous job and who still seemed to be at the centre of the most recent secret reports and assessments he had now been studying. He decided to send a carefully coded signal to his successor in London, Andrei Volkov, to produce an update on the activities of the MI5 Operations Director, Tom Spencer.

The first report surprised Rozovsky – "Spencer has recently retired from MI5 and to date we have been unable to trace any current information about his activities or location."

After scrutinising all the existing files relating to the MI5 man and looking carefully for any hidden clues, he decided to discuss the matter again with his Director, Yuri Bortsov. "I think I should go to London myself and work on this one," he began.

He went on to remind Bortsov that it was Spencer who had personally travelled to Portsmouth to detain Aldanov on that ill-fated mission to create a new informant in the British navy. Then Aldanov had been grilled face to face by Spencer before his first court appearance and then his transfer to a secure jail to wait for an espionage trial.

Rozovsky continued: "And then came the death of the woman dated by Aldanov and the murder charges against our two agents who had been sent to find her and left Ricin in her mailbox. I knew that Spencer was still on the case, but our intelligence was good and our two agents had already left the country. At least we got that one right. Then there was the strange episode of the woman's funeral and I decided to find a way to be there to see who was involved. It was not just a family affair, but the top Navy people were also there and so were a couple of MI5 officers, including Spencer again. I became even more suspicious and as I walked away, I was stopped by Spencer and taken to a police car – and then spent two years in jail. And meanwhile, as you know, there was the unexpected spy swap and Aldanov's return to Moscow – probably masterminded by Spencer and all with a great deal of embarrassing publicity".

Birtsov then interrupted: "And while you were in jail, it seems that Volkov's boys messed up another assignment which was intended to get Spencer when he went to Portsmouth again. That event is described here in the files as the unveiling of a memorial to Aldanov's mystery woman. According to the reports, they missed the target and managed to get a Ricin gun hit on Spencer's female assistant. Those two agents are still locked up there for attempted murder and you know the rest."

"Well, we can't win them all – so let's get him this time," was Rozovsky's brief reply.

"I realise that this is personal for you," replied Bortsov. "But we did manage to get you back after a couple of years and the last thing we want at the moment is another incident with the press digging up all the background again. I think you would be a marked man if you turned up in London and I need you here. So see if you can work it out with Volkov – he is a good operator and he now has some experienced agents in his team".

Rozovsky reluctantly agreed and said he would keep his boss informed – and immediately went to work on developing a plan. This required Volkov and his team to focus all their efforts on a discrete search for clues relating to Spencer among all their contacts and to cross-reference any possible snippets of information. To emphasise the importance of the assignment, he told Volkov: "We have to find a way to eliminate this man."

A week later, an update was beginning to be assembled. It emerged that Spencer had travelled abroad after leaving his London apartment which was now empty and on the market. His mail forwarding address was care of his brother, Bernard Spencer, in Scotland. The research also described the brother as a well-known TV cameraman who had worked on programmes exploring wildlife in South America and Africa. Armed with this information, the Russian agents in London were instructed by Volkov to drive to Scotland as tourists, locate the brother's address and find a way to discretely observe the comings and goings there for a few days.

It did not take long before they were able to report that there was indeed a recent new arrival at the address who seemed to be in residence, together with a woman. They were getting attention from the locals because of their spectacular silver Lamborghini car and according to the gossip in the village pub, it was Bernard Spencer's rich brother from London.

Rosovsky reviewed all the information carefully and deduced that the expensive car was consistent with a lifelong bachelor receiving a handsome bonus on his retirement and then using it to impress a woman friend as well as his brother. In a confidential discussion, Volkov added: "My guys are staying in the area as tourists walking in the mountains. They are staying at a nearby guest house and the locals have told them about the arrival of a large delivery truck belonging to a London company of furniture removers. So maybe our man is moving in?"

"That sounds good. My hunch tells me you have found the right man," replied Rozovsky from Moscow. "Can they check his movements and see if there is a suitable opportunity to strike? What gear do they have with them?"

Told that they were equipped with small quantities of poisons and explosives he ended the call and went immediately to report the progress to his Birtsov, his Director. "Do I need authority to go ahead with the kill?" he asked.

"No – we missed him once so let's do it right this time," was the succinct response.

Just three days later, the Russian agents watched as "Tom and Mary" parked their impressive car as usual in the car park of the village pub for a quick drink among new friends before lunch. It was a quiet day in the village, and the couple did not notice the white 4x4 vehicle which followed them a minute or two later and parked a few spaces away. The two men in the vehicle waited a while until the coast was clear and then quickly carried out a well-practised discrete action to place an explosive device under the Lamborghini, beneath the driver's seat, equipped to detonate when the vehicle's ignition was started. They then drove away and parked again at a nearby location with a clear view of the car park and waited ...

They watched the couple leave the bar about ten minutes later, and those inside the bar rushed outside on hearing an explosion and were shocked to see the expensive sports car in flames and torn apart. Several vehicles parked nearby were badly damaged by the blast but fortunately there were no casualties apart from the charred bodies of the couple which could not be reached until the police and emergency services arrived. By then, the Russia spooks had already driven off on their pre-planned route using minor roads which avoided any security or speed cameras – and sent a coded "job done" message to Volkov at the London embassy. When the news reached Bortsov in Moscow, he eagerly reported to the Minister that his four-point revenge plan had been completed - but he did not know that his other elusive target of "a mystery female CIA agent" had also been eliminated.

During the police and security service investigations in Scotland, a security camera at the pub car park eventually provided evidence to identify the white vehicle parked next to the Lamborghini and the two men who planted the fatal bomb. The van had been rented in London a week earlier and was then traced to the car park at Aberdeen railway station. It was assumed that the assassins had succeeded in escaping from the area unrecognised and no doubt they had expertly flown out of the country before the police or MI5 could catch up with them.

The local residents, and indeed the whole of Scotland, were aghast at what had happened in this quiet corner of the country. There was little for the police investigation to discover and the follow-up murder inquiry was taken over by experts from MI5 as a terrorism hit and they gave little away in response to questions from the media. The two perpetrators were identified as known GUR agents and the inquest in Aberdeen confirmed the identities of the two victims as Sir Thomas and Lady Spencer. The cause of death was the inevitable verdict of "murder by person or persons unknown".

There were no VIP's at the simple funeral for Tom and Mary some three weeks later at the village church where Tom's parents had been buried – just an anonymous stranger from London who was accompanying the local police chief. Bernard Spencer's eulogy on behalf of the family described his early years and educational achievements, leading to a successful career in the Civil Service. He gave little away and concluded – "My brother has been cruelly deprived of the retirement he deserved after a long career in the service of his country". Afterwards, a short government statement was issued, which paid tribute to "the tragic death of a retired senior officer from the Ministry of Defence, Sir Thomas Spencer together with Lady Spencer in a terrorism incident in Scotland" and thanked him for his years of service to the country. MI5 succeeded in minimising the follow up press coverage of the incident which mainly concentrated on interviews with those who were in the pub on the fatal day – and expressing their sadness from the villagers at the loss of "Tom and Mary", their newest neighbours.

In the following days, there was just a handful of top Royal Navy, Police and MI5 officials in Portsmouth and London, all bound by the official secrets act, who understood much, much more.

And each in their own way, the small group who knew all the facts could only think, simply and sadly: "Farewell to Marina – again".

Chapter 38

Russia On the Offensive

The secret services of the UK and USA had been sharing new information from their sources in Moscow for several weeks which had persuaded them that there was a hardening of attitudes in the Kremlin. The security agency directors on both sides of the Atlantic had not been too surprised by the two incidents in the UK – at the American Embassy and at the Porton Research Centre. They hooked up on a hot-line each day with other key staff – and they quickly agreed that these raids were the work of the GRU, and probably directed from within the small group based at the embassy in London.

Then, during one of their now more frequent video conferences, the directors and senior staff of the two agencies were interrupted by an official from the London security service who handed a one-page document to "M". There was silence for a minute or so as he read it and then told the group in sombre tones: "I am sorry to say there has been another tragic incident. This time it's in Scotland where a car bomb has killed our recently retired Operations Director at MI5 – a brilliant man called Tom Spencer. Many of you knew him, of course, and we will find out more later. But this is terrible news for those of us who worked with Spencer".

He paused as heads were lowered around the room, and then continued: "I will share any more details when I received them. At the very least, I think the coincidence of timing is crucial and I suspect that the influence of Rozovsky was involved in the planning of all these UK operations. We have suffered two fatal attacks with high grade miniature incendiary devices and now this targeted assassination of Tom Spencer – plus that shooting of the Russian in Washington. But it concerns me that we did not have any specific advance intelligence about any of these deadly actions, not even about the purchase of drones. We need to study this carefully and find ways to improve our sources."

Details of the latest sad news from Scotland and the other developments were distributed immediately to the key ministers and there was heightened urgency when another COBRA meeting was convened later that day with the Prime Minister in the chair. Three Cabinet Ministers took their seats in the briefing room, together with the American Ambassador, "M" and other senior civil servants and intelligence officials plus the chief of the armed forces and the Commissioner of the Metropolitan Police.

There was much gloom and sadness following a detailed report on the latest incident in Scotland and the Prime Minister led the group to observe a minute of silent respect followed by a brief appreciation from "M" of Tom Spencer's career.

Then returning to business, "M" reported that his team had been monitoring an increasing volume of coded communications activity between Moscow and London in recent days. They were also following up on the activities and background of at least one experienced new Russian agent who had arrived to join the GRU team at their London embassy. They had suspected that something new was being planned – but had not identified anything specific. They had now concluded that it was more than a coincidence that these recent activities had followed the recent return to Moscow of the jailed senior diplomat Rozovsky in the spy swap for the businessman's wife. The UK team had therefore been analysing the information he might have taken back to Russia from his previous two years of experience in the London embassy.

Henry Burbeck, the American ambassador had been invited to the meeting to update on the situation following the incident at his residence, and he asked whether the release of the jailed diplomat had in fact been such a good idea? The Prime Minister replied: "At the time, it seemed like a good solution to a rather embarrassing incident following the detention in Moscow of the wife of one of our high visibility business leaders. With the benefit of hindsight, you are probably right, Henry. But the connection with these tragic events is somewhat circumstantial, I think."

"I am not so sure," came a thoughtful intervention from "M", adding: "I now think the whole spy swap was probably a Russian set-up job to get the return of their man Rozovsky and we fell for it."

The Foreign Secretary then reported that the Russian Ambassador had been summoned to the Foreign Office again that morning, adding: "Not surprisingly, he has denied all knowledge of these three incidents and has suggested that the bomb attacks were the result of terrorist activities. And when I told him about the discovery of Russian-made incendiary devices in Wiltshire, he suggested that terrorists would know how to obtain these and how to deliver them against targets which might then appear to be the work of Russia. He was as usual very dour and dismissive, and he reluctantly accepted the official letter from the PM. I told him to expect further repercussions from both the American and British governments – and that was about it."

Ambassador Burbeck added that a similar protest had been lodged at the Russian embassy in Washington and the ambassador had been summoned to the State Department. He also proposed that the two governments should jointly seek the support of both NATO and the European Union in their responses and that they should urgently conside further actions in response to these attacks.

The Prime Minister said he agreed wholeheartedly and turning to "M" again, he asked: "After all this, is there anything else we should know?"

"Yes, quite a lot, sir," came the purposeful reply. And the group focussed their attention on him as he continued, slowly and emphatically:

"Together with our colleagues in the States, we have been preparing a detailed joint assessment of the sea change which seems to be occurring in Moscow's military and security activities. We believe these latest missions by the GRU are just a pin prick to send a message to the West. These have been relatively small attacks which they were able to plan and carry out covertly and without any military involvement – and together with this latest assassination in Scotland, we believe that the actions are intended to demonstrate that Russia is now on the offensive and testing our reactions. As I reported briefly at an earlier meeting, there are some significant troop movements taking place within Russia which clearly show a new and evolving policy to demonstrate their strengths. I believe that we and our allies need to review our strategic plans and our military resources accordingly."

There were murmurs of agreement from the key people around the table and the mood became sombre as the American ambassador added: "This cannot wait for the next planned meetings of NATO. I will advise my masters in Washington to convene a joint action group on all this without delay".

The others agreed and the British intelligence chief ended the meeting by telling the COBRA group: "We know that the bear is stirring and that we in the West are their targets".

"We have urgent work to do, but we will be ready – and more" was the confident pronouncement by the Prime Minister as he stood up and briskly led the way out of the room.

And then ....?

Printed in Great Britain
by Amazon

15925917R00122